OUR FAVORITE SONGS

A MOONLIGHTERS NOVELLA

ANITA KELLY

D1073046

NOTE TO READERS

This novella includes mention of parental death from cancer, brain cancer specifically, as well as one line referencing self-harm. Please treat yourselves with care.

For Lou
who listened to Radiohead with me &
helped me feel a little less alone in high school

& for the OG Anita
you are missed

1

AIDEN

"Of course," Kai Andrews said as he sat down across from me. "It's you."

Kai Andrews.

Just sat down.

Across from me.

I did a quick memory check to make sure I wasn't high.

Alas, the only depressant I'd consumed tonight was this just-okay IPA in front of me. And Kai Andrews was definitely still sitting at my table, snug against the back wall of Moonie's, next to the sole window in the building. Like most squat buildings containing exactly one window, Moonie's—or The Moonlight Café, if you wanted to be technical about it, and nobody did—wasn't a particularly fancy place. A fact only doubly confirmed by said window being mostly obscured by black bars and a large neon sign advertising Bud Light.

But still, it was my shitty bar, my barely-a-window window, my slightly crooked table. Where I was supposed to be meeting Penelope, my best friend, for our semiannual let's-get-drunk-and-laugh-at-people-doing-karaoke Moonie's invitational.

Which my high school nemesis had definitely never, ever been invited to.

Kai laughed. Or half-laughed. It was one of those charming, head-shaking kind of quiet chuckles that only truly attractive people could pull off.

"I take it Pen didn't tell you she invited me."

My mouth, which I presumed had been gaping like a fish, snapped shut. I grabbed my smudgy pint glass and drew my just-okay beer closer to myself, as if it could protect me.

"Yeah, that'd be a *no*."

Of course Kai was laughing. Of course he thought this was funny.

He tilted his head. A strand of shiny russet hair shifted on his perfect forehead.

"Wow. Aiden. You are like...seriously pissed. I didn't know either, that you'd be here. If that helps."

"It's fine," I said, even though it wasn't; it was *weird*, so weird, that he was here, that Pen did not run this by me. But *it's fine* was what normal people said in these kinds of situations, and I was totally going to be normal about this. I was not freaking out. "What are you even doing in the city? Don't you live down south somewhere now?"

Kai shook his head, brought his own pint glass, full of something clear and bubbly, to his lips.

"Not anymore. Just got a job at the port."

"Oh. What are you doing, building ships or something?"

Kai placed his glass carefully back on the table, clearing his throat.

"Welding on them. Yes."

Let it be noted, for the record, that I did not disintegrate into goo here, even though I wanted to.

Of course Kai Andrews was building ships. It helped explain the fact that he was more built than ever. He was currently hiding most of his bulk under a thick hoodie, considering it was approximately ten degrees outside, but I could *tell*. His shoulders were even more lumberjack-y than they had been in high school. I didn't want to think about what his biceps looked like under there.

His face was the same. Almost. It was probably point-five degrees more handsome. Which was infuriating.

"So. What are you up to these days, McCarstle?"

Waiting for Penelope to show up and explain herself to me.

"I'm…" I faltered, the gears of my brain still struggling to shift from first to second. And anyway, I truly could not think of anything I wanted to do less at this moment than tell Kai Andrews, Ship Builder and Owner of the Perfect Face, about my MFA. "I'm in grad school." *And walking dogs on the side. I don't know how I'm existing, or how I even afforded this beer, to be honest. Aren't I impressive?*

"For writing?"

"Yeah." I scowled.

Kai's face actually lit up with a smile. Like he was proud of me.

"That's awesome. What are you writing these days? Still…"

And because we lived in a reckless, cruel world, the earth did not swallow me up into a pleasant dark hole when I said, "Poetry. Yeah."

Kai's smile stretched wider. His skin was flawless, his teeth straight as sin.

"Awesome," he said again. "I can't wait until I can buy your books at Barnes & Noble one day and say, hey, I knew that guy once."

We had known each other, once. Barely. We knew each other because, for whatever reason, Penelope loved both of us, and we loved her. Because Penelope was the rarest of flowers, a tropical bird: grace and blinding colors, a magical ability to flit between all social groups and leave everyone somehow better in her wake.

Kai Andrews, though, solidly fit into one box. Star soccer player. Handsome, polite. Didn't overload on AP classes like me, but still made the honor roll. He was the kind of teenager teachers would bring up in the staff room whenever he won his latest accolade, pointing at each other and saying, "Kai Andrews? Now, that's a good kid." Top Candidate for Goodest Kid.

I was pretty sure Kai had done an apprenticeship after high school. Like it was the fucking 1800s or something. That was the level of pure he was.

And I was the gangly queer boy who scribbled poetry in the margins of all of my notebooks. Who detested extracurricular activities, mainly because I was never brave enough to join one. A mid-tier candidate for Smart Awkward Kid We'll All Forget About in a Year.

And now, five years post high school graduation, somehow we were sitting at a tiny table together at The Moonlight Café. If there was anywhere I pictured ever running into Kai Andrews again, it certainly wasn't this odd, queer karaoke bar in a deserted corner of the city. His presence made me feel off kilter, like the filter on the world had just changed and my eyes were still adjusting. His knee brushed against mine and I nearly jumped.

"Don't hold your breath," I eventually mustered. About the finding me in Barnes & Noble thing. Which had been a very Dad thing to say, like he should have been ruffling my hair as he said it. Kai Andrews was a built, hot dad, and having him in front of me made me feel like a teenager again. Running a little too hot, not knowing what to do with my hands.

And then, thank god, my phone rang.

Penelope was FaceTiming.

Which, I realized with a sinking feeling in my gut, was not a good sign—her face should be here, at Moonie's, and not inside the cracked screen of my phone—but I swiped to pick up anyway.

And saw my best friend sitting in a hospital bed. With a big white bandage on her forehead.

"Hey! Hey hey hey hey," she said, fast, before I could even open my mouth.

"Pen?" I frowned, leaning in to hear her over the din of Moonie's. It was still pretty dead in here, but she sounded too tinny and far away anyway. "What happened?"

Kai leaned over the table, trying to see her too. Which brought his perfect face entirely too close to mine. I tried to position the screen at the center of the table between us, to prevent any further leaning on his part, but it didn't seem to help matters.

"So, little thing, not a big deal, I promise, just—oh, hey! Kai! You made it!"

Her face burst with a smile, bandage shifting as her eyebrows catapulted.

"I did. Can you tell us why you, on the other hand, appear to be at the hospital?"

"Well, okay, I was on my way there, I swear, but did you all know the rain turned into snow? And apparently there was black ice? And my tires did a wee little whoopseedaisie and—" Kai and I both leaned in even closer as she paused. His hair almost brushed my cheek. "And I might have had a slight run in with one of those signs that flash at you how fast you're going over the speed limit? Which, if you think about it, is kind of funny. Like I was finally just like, 'fuck you, sign!'"

Kai, the heathen, actually did laugh, another soft chuckle. I frowned, increasingly concerned about Pen. Glancing out the window, I could just barely see, through the bars and the back of the Bud Light sign, a smidge of the parking lot, where—huh—snow was indeed funneling through the air, highlighted by the bright spotlights of the lot.

"Penelope," I said. "What happened after you hit the pole?"

"Well, first, this woman stopped and was like, 'whoa,' and I was like 'I know,' and it really is true, you know, how when bad things happen, the helpers are always there, or whatever Mr. Rogers says, and—"

Penelope paused again. I could see, even through my cracked screen, her lip begin to quiver.

"Pen," I said, trying not to grow frustrated, being that she had a big bandage on her head.

"He was so good, you know?" She wiped at her eyes. "He was such a good man. We need a new Mr. Rogers. Like, right now."

"I know we do," I soothed. "But Pen, what happened to you after that? Are you okay?"

"Yes, I'm fine, honestly. My knee's a little crushed and I guess I bonked my head and I have a tiny bit of a concussion. And my ribs hurt a little? But seriously, I'm lucky I was just going down Division and not, like, 405."

"Hey, Penelope?" Kai cut in. "I love you, and I'm glad you're feeling okay, but I'm pretty sure you're not supposed to be using screens, if you have a concussion?"

"Oh, right, absolutely. Mikey's on his way and he'll do his growly thing if he sees me doing this. But I knew Aiden couldn't be truly mad at me if he saw my poor concussed face on video."

I opened my mouth to defend myself.

"Well," I said.

Master of Fine Arts, right here.

"I'm so sorry I didn't tell you Kai was coming!" Penelope yelled, all her words running together, and I didn't know if this frenzied shout was because of the blunt trauma to her head, or a practiced effort to make me less upset.

"I knew Kai wouldn't care if you were there, but I was worried you would say no. I decided to not say anything, in case the night fell through anyway, but...I've been trying to meet back up with Kai since he got back into town. And I haven't seen *you* in like, three weeks, either, Aiden, and I miss you, both of you, and I had all these ice breakers in my back pocket I was going to use, and—was he mad, Kai?"

"Oh, yeah," Kai grinned. "Like, *super* mad."

"I was *surprised*," I clarified, glaring at both of them. "A reasonable response, I think."

"Anyway," Kai said smoothly, "I really think you should go before Mikey, or the nurses, yell at you for being on FaceTime. Can you ask Mikey to text one of us when you get home?"

"Aye, Captain." She saluted. "And listen, I really am sorry for causing this cluster, but maybe you should both just head out? Get home safe? You know our city doesn't know how to handle snow."

"Yeah," Kai said. "We'll take care of ourselves. Love you."

"Love you, too." A pause. "Aiden?"

Oh. Right. "Love you, too."

Penelope blew a kiss, and was gone.

I flipped the phone screen down on the table and sat back in my chair, blowing out a breath. I stared out the window. This city of rain really was a mess when it came to snow. The fact that it was snowing at all right now was so typical. Snowstorms forecasted for weeks never materialized; snow no one expected shut down the city for days.

We should go.

Except...I was feeling embarrassed, somehow. I loved Pen, and clearly she knew me too well, but—*I knew Kai wouldn't care if you were there, but I was worried you would say no.* The fact that she had to keep it from me, and then call me on FaceTime, while concussed, to make sure I wasn't too mad. Which was a smart move, but still.

I wasn't a child. I could be a grownup about this. Kai and I were hanging out now. This was fine. And the snow wasn't even sticking yet. Or at least, I didn't think so. It was hard to tell what the outside world actually looked like through the Bud Light haze.

I looked at him. He had leaned back in his chair too, a much more acceptable distance between our faces again. I realized the silence had probably been stretching too long. He had an eyebrow raised in question, and it was super hot. Were my facial muscles even capable of quirking a brow like that? God.

"Well," I said again, my newest favorite word. I steeled my spine a bit. I could handle this. "We're already here. We might as well finish our drinks."

Kai stared back at me for a moment. It was possible I could actively feel my pits sweating, during that moment, but that was a plus of being at Moonie's. It already smelled kind of weird in here.

"Sure," he said eventually, wrapping his hand around his pint glass, all of his calloused fingers, his wonderful, knuckley knuckles.

I had this sudden flashback. Junior year of high school, I had overslept and was incredibly late to school. I was rushing to first period and my backpack just...broke. Like the zipper just fucking broke, out of nowhere, and my shit went everywhere.

And of course—*of course*, like it was a dumb teen movie —Kai Andrews was there. Somehow having chosen that exact moment to step into the hall on his way to the bathroom. So we were both scrambling to pick up all of my papers and books, and I couldn't believe it was actually happening the whole time. We kept reaching for the same things at the same time, so our hands kept bumping into each other, fingers brushing, knuckles knocking, and it was simultaneously the most mortifying and erotic experience of my young adult life. It probably took five minutes to clean up my stuff, but it felt like an hour, at least. And at one point, Kai shook his head and said, almost under his breath: "God, you're such a mess."

It was possible I went home and cried. And then maybe wrote a poem about Kai Andrews's knuckles.

He picked up his glass now and gave me a small smile.

"Sounds like a plan to me."

2

KAI

I HATED how relieved I was, when Aiden didn't want to bolt at the first opportunity. It was snowing; Penelope was in the hospital. There was no reason to be here.

And yet.

I was glad Aiden didn't want to leave.

Which was...annoying.

I didn't know why this guy still irked me so much. Why it *mattered* that he still clearly hated me. Or maybe he didn't *hate* me. Was irritated by me. Actively disliked me. Did not want to be bothered by my presence.

And for some reason, even though I hadn't talked to him in five years, I still wanted him to change his mind.

It really hadn't been a surprise to me, when I walked in and saw the back of his head slouched over this table, that tightly curled black hair as unkempt as ever, the pale stretch of his neck above his sweater so oddly familiar. I knew he and Pen were still close. She would mention hanging out with him in our texts, or he'd pop up on her Instagram sometimes. Half of me maybe even expected him to be here.

But when I actually saw Aiden McCarstle in front of me, I felt almost...excited. That maybe he'd see me this time, years later, and for once in his goddamn life, he'd smile. Hold out his hand and say, "Hey, man. How's it going? Good to see you."

But of course, he'd only scowled. Exactly like he'd scowled every time I even glanced his way in high school.

I just didn't *get* it. I was always nice to him. I tried to be nice to everybody. I didn't think it would have bothered me if he was simply a jerk, another snooty smart kid rolling his eyes at the jock. Who cared.

But I knew Pen, and she wasn't friends with jerks. She loved Aiden McCarstle with her whole being.

There was also the fact that I'd read every poem he'd ever published in our school's literary magazine. And there was that time we were in pre-calc together senior year and sat next to each other, and I might have glanced at his notebook sometimes. Because he was always scribbling something. And somehow still easily managed an A. I worked harder than I'd ever worked at anything in that class to muster by with a B-. Aiden spent half of every class writing stanzas in his notebooks that had nothing to do with logarithms or exponential functions, and still kicked my ass.

Point was, his poems were always really good.

It made me inordinately happy, actually, that he was still working on writing stuff. That Aiden McCarstle hadn't turned into an accountant or something. Not that there was anything wrong with being an accountant. If pre-calc was any indication, he would have been good at that, too. It just wouldn't have felt right, for him.

Anyway, it was just...weird. That he wrote all these pretty things, but still scowled at me so much.

Even though he wasn't scowling at me anymore. He

had been kind of curled into himself, after he'd hung up with Penelope, in that way he always used to sit, staring out the window and unconsciously messing with a loose string on the sleeve of his sweater. It was black and white striped, the sweater, a little loose on Aiden, who was as skinny as ever. His face was a little leaner, a little sharper. His eyes a little older. But otherwise, he looked exactly the same.

He straightened now, tall and severe in his seat. Really *looked* at me. Like he was ready to do this now. Whatever *this* was.

And only then did it finally, finally occur to me.

I had to fight to not laugh.

Ever since I'd realized I was bi a few years ago, I'd been going through old memories in my head, trying to figure out when I should have known. All the things I'd hidden from myself. Realized I had probably been half in love with my co-captain on the team, Lars, for years. That really, a large majority of my entire soccer career from my first middle school camp through senior year had been slightly homoerotic.

McCarstle had never even crossed my mind.

But I saw it now, as I looked at his ratty sweater and those dark eyes staring me down from that assessing, intelligent face.

It had always bothered me that Aiden never liked me because Pen loved him and because he wrote really beautiful words. But I'd only just received the last piece of the puzzle, the one I hadn't been ready to admit to myself in high school.

I'd always thought he was kind of cute.

Oh my god. I was a shallow jock, after all.

I'd been pretty damn positive about the bisexual thing for at least three years now, but man. Rewriting the history you thought you'd known never ceased to be mind-blowing. And *hilarious*.

All this time, I'd had a crush on this guy and never even knew.

I leaned back and took another sip of my Sprite to hide my smile.

Moving back home had been harder, and weirder, and lonelier than I'd expected. I was going to let myself enjoy this night.

"So," I said, "We should probably figure out what we're going to sing."

Aiden's Very Serious Exterior he'd been giving me broke suddenly, a slash of panic crossing his face.

"What? No, you must've misheard me. I only said we'd finish a drink. We're not...I don't sing."

I tilted my head at him.

"You hang out at a karaoke bar, and you don't sing? Still trying *that* hard to not have fun, McCarstle?"

He frowned, forehead creasing.

He opened his mouth, and then snapped it shut. Full on glared at me. Which tickled something in my gut, made me want to laugh again. Did I *like* it when he looked angry with me? I guess I had needled him a bit there. Attraction was confusing.

Abruptly, Aiden stood and stalked across the room. He talked with the cute girl who had recently moved behind the high table in the corner, stationing herself behind a laptop. It was hard to tell from here, and Aiden only paused at the table for a minute at most, but I was pretty sure he smiled at her, his shoulders relaxing an inch as she smiled back.

Okay, no. I definitely still wanted him to smile at me.

When he returned, he threw a few small pieces of paper, along with two tiny golf pencils, onto the table.

"Fine," he said. "Let's do this. But I have a proposition. We get to choose the song the other person has to sing."

I smiled, grabbing a paper and one of the pencils.

"I'm game. So are we choosing songs the other would hate? Or think was funny, or something?"

"Yes," Aiden said, hunched over, already scribbling on his, one hand covering the paper, as if this was a school quiz and he thought I might cheat. He added, "Or whatever you want."

"And we don't tell each other what we chose."

"No." He flipped over his paper and sat back in his chair, crossing his arms over his chest.

I tapped my pencil against the slightly sticky tabletop. Suddenly, the options seemed limitless. There were simply so many songs Aiden McCarstle probably hated.

After a second, Aiden left the table again. I liked watching him march across the room, in those skinny dark jeans and that sweater that was definitely too big for him.

He plopped a huge black binder on the table.

"If you need inspiration," he said, before grabbing his beer and staring out the window again.

I flipped through the plastic pages, and holy shit, the options actually *were* limitless. This was more stressful than I anticipated. But then my eyes landed on something in the Cs, and it just seemed right, for Mr. Tortured Artist over there. It was a good song. And yeah, he'd probably hate it.

I wrote it down. Without looking at it, Aiden snatched up both pieces of paper and brought them up to the cute girl. He sighed when he sat back down.

"I might need more alcohol for this."

"I'll grab the next round," I said, standing. "What kind of beer are you drinking?"

I expected him to scowl again in protest, but he only nodded. "Whatever IPA's on tap. That'd be nice, thanks."

Having survived another visit with the intimidating butch bartender I'd met when I first walked into the bar, I returned to the table with two more pint glasses. I had been trying to think, the whole time I waited at the bar, of conversation starters that would help Aiden McCarstle not hate me. If Pen hadn't been concussed, I might have texted her for some of those ice breakers.

But before I even had a chance to try, Aiden surprised me.

"I heard about your mom, last year. I'm sorry."

I blinked.

"Oh." I took a sip of my soda. "Yeah. Thanks."

It had been a brain tumor. She'd been totally fine, preparing to retire and live her best life. And then within a year, she was gone. Just like that.

It was part of the reason I'd moved back home, to deal with the house. Aunt Tina had done a little bit, but I'd offered to do the rest. It was too much for Dad. And I wanted to do it.

I just didn't know why I hadn't done it sooner. The truth was, I'd wanted to turn around and come back home pretty much the moment I set foot in Klamath Falls five years ago. But I was learning so much at the forge down there, where I apprenticed, and they kept promoting me, and...I don't know. I learned how easy it was, sometimes, to get stuck in a place.

I should have moved back the moment Mom got the diagnosis. I came back a lot for visits, to check in during treatments, but I kept going back to Klamath Falls to "wrap things up," even though wrapping things up usually meant staring into space after work, rubbing my dog Jack's ears, and doing absolutely nothing. And then she was gone. I finally came back for good then.

For some reason, I came back after she'd already died. And I'd never be able to explain why.

"Sorry if that was weird, to bring it up," Aiden said, shifting in his seat. "I just remembered, all of a sudden, Penelope telling me about it."

"No," I said. "It's okay. I'm glad you did. Most people I know simply pretend it never happened, so. It's good, to acknowledge that it did."

"Yeah." Aiden nodded.

And all of my conversation starters had disappeared out of my head, now. But I felt oddly more comfortable. I meant what I'd said; I actually was glad Aiden had mentioned it. It brought us a little more up to speed with each other, in the here and now of our post-high school realities. And it made me feel a little better about him, that he cared enough to remember Pen telling him about it, that he cared enough to say something.

In general, I'd learned I could always breathe a little better, whenever someone did mention Mom. Like the grief moved partially out into the open air instead of existing solely in my brain. Always hurt more, but still gave me more space to breathe anyway.

"So Mikey," I said, after another long sip of my drink. "I haven't actually met him yet. He a good guy?"

"Oh," Aiden's eyebrows lifted at the change in topic, but his shoulders relaxed, like they had when he'd talked to the karaoke jockey. "Yeah. He's great, actually. They met that summer when Pen worked at Trader Joe's?" A small wash of pink graced the tops of his cheeks. "Sorry, you probably know that already."

"No, it's okay," I shook my head. "I haven't been around; it's different. I only get the texted version of things, or the Instagram version of things. I want to know."

"Yeah. Okay. He's kind of goofy. Like, would gladly wear those Hawaiian shirts even when he wasn't at the store, you know?" Aiden shrugged. "But I don't know; he's really sweet. Loves Pen a lot."

"He sounds perfect for her."

"Yeah." Aiden grinned a little into his beer, and my stomach swooped. It was the first time his lips had curved that way, at least in front of me, since I first sat down. And it was lovely.

"All right, friends who have endured this fine wintry mix out here to join us tonight!"

The cute KJ boomed over the room on the mic. My head swiveled automatically toward her and the large dance floor next to her station, a disco ball shining neon lights onto its empty surface.

"Time to get the party started with everyone's favorite Moonie's performer...Lily!"

A woman wearing an aqua colored dress decorated with large purple polka dots walked to the dance floor, taking the mic and launching into a rather impressive rendition of "Before He Cheats."

She made me smile, all of her bright colors and her swagger.

Her joy also made me start to doubt my song choice for McCarstle.

Aiden made an *a-ha* sound in his throat, and I turned back to him, an eyebrow raised in question.

"Oh, sorry. I just realized something. It's not important at all. But this woman's partner, over there." He pointed with his chin toward a person sitting along the wall, who was staring at the blonde woman singing Carrie Underwood like they wanted to eat her. "They've looked kind of familiar every time I'm here, and it just clicked. I think they're a professor at my school. I've never had them, but

I've seen them around. Anyway. Now I know where they get their fashion sense."

I could see what he meant. The professor wore a skirt that wasn't as colorful as Lily's dress, but still chic in its own way.

"What school do you go to?" I turned back toward Aiden.

"Oh, just the university downtown." He slumped back into his chair again.

"And...grad school," I said slowly, realizing I knew absolutely nothing about grad school. "Is that a full-time thing? Or do you work somewhere too?"

He ran a hand over his face, like even the mention of school exhausted him.

"Yeah, it's pretty full-time, but I do...um. I walk dogs, on the side."

I almost choked on my Sprite.

"You walk dogs?"

He blushed fully now, and it was so pretty, that heat filling the sharp lines of his face.

"Yes," he said, sounding distinctly irritated again, and I seriously had to stop being turned on by that. "I don't know if you remember Amy Bishop, from school? She runs her own dog walking business, and..." He shrugged. "It helps pay the rent. Sometimes."

God, I was tickled by this. I wondered what McCarstle's favorite kind of dog was. I pictured him holding a wiggly, snot-nosed puggle up to his serious face, and I couldn't even hold in my smile.

We watched two other people perform. The first chose an old Blink-182 song, which made me laugh, while the other shouted a slightly cringey version of "Single Ladies." We continued to make small talk. I was beginning to feel pretty good, like maybe Aiden McCarstle didn't completely hate me, after all.

And then the KJ called his name.

3

"Hurt."

As written by Trent Reznor. As performed by Johnny fucking Cash.

Otherwise known as the most depressing thing ever fucking recorded.

Who even performed "Hurt" at karaoke? Someone who was able to sound like Johnny Cash, maybe, but let me tell you, that wasn't me, and otherwise it was only awkward. I was already up here, and I had a mic in my hand, and I had promised myself to act like a fucking adult, so I wasn't going to stomp out of the room like a pissed off child, even though I was definitely pissed off.

So I sang. If you could count trying to get through this miserable song as singing, which I didn't. It was elongating syllables in the most painful way possible. In front of a room full of strangers. It was possible I'd never be able to return to Moonie's again.

I had no idea what song I'd thought Kai would choose for me, but I definitely hadn't expected *this*. Did he think I was that much of a cliché? Did he think I still sat in my room listening to shit like this and smoking clove cigarettes?

And to think I'd actually started to feel a little soft toward him, after I'd remembered his mom had died. After we'd managed twenty minutes of acceptable conversation. After he started looking at me in this way that was...faintly intriguing.

Of course, I hadn't seen the guy in five years. Maybe I forgot some details about him. Maybe that was how he looked at everyone.

Not that it mattered how Kai Andrews looked at me, anyway.

In any case, I felt like a dumb joke for every excruciating minute of that song, and I'd been wrong. Kai Andrews wasn't the goodest kid. He was an asshole.

I returned the mic to Kiki without looking her in the eye and stomped over to the bar. I still had half of my beer back at the table, and I didn't know if I could truly afford that many more drinks on my own tab, but the bar was as far away as I could currently get from Kai. Plus, the bartender here was the best. Maybe if I had a minute of being surrounded by her badass, cold-as-ice vibe it'd help me put myself back together again.

"Another?" she asked.

"Yeah." I pushed my palms against the edge of the bar.

"That was a weird song choice, man."

I shook my head, sighed.

"Yeah."

"I liked it."

I met her silver-blue eyes over the taps. She nodded and shoved the beer my way. As soon as I grabbed it she turned back to her till, dismissing me.

Yeah. That had helped.

I took a sip off the top before squaring my shoulders. Nothing for it.

I fell back into my seat across from Kai. Who at least had the good sense to look chagrined.

"Hey," he said immediately, leaning forward, "Aiden, I—"

"And now, good folks of The Moonlight Café," Kiki sang into her mic. "Help me welcome up to the stage…Kai!"

Kai's lips set into a fine line before he stood.

I leaned back in my seat, downing the rest of my beer(s).

Maybe watching Kai also humiliate himself would make the night a bit better. And then I could go home, and pretend this had all been a strange fever dream.

But of course not.

Because while Kai's face still looked tense as he walked onto the dance floor, soon, the dulcet tones of Miley Cyrus's "Party in the USA" burst out of the speakers. And Kai's face morphed into an easy, relaxed grin.

He jumped into the first verse right on beat.

He got more into it with every single line. Started boogying around the floor, his smile somehow perpetually growing. He…seemed to know every word? Like, he was barely looking at the screen. He rubbed his stomach, hunched over his shoulders when Miley talked about being nervous, homesick. During the first chorus, he threw the hand that wasn't holding the mic in the air, waved it around like he just didn't care.

He was having the time of his life.

Fuck me.

I didn't know why I thought it would be funny to watch him sing a song like this. The only song I knew for certain that Kai Andrews loved was a real weird one from the '70s or '80s or something, so I thought a solid 2000s pop tune would be a decent choice for prime embarrassment, especially for someone like him. Someone made of bulging biceps and knuckles that made me shiver. But of course. Of course Kai Andrews was the one all-American boy somehow bred without a shred of toxic masculinity.

And the crowd was loving it. Well, if you could call it a crowd. The bar was half empty, probably because of the snow. Still, everyone else present, except for me and the bartender, emptied their seats, the butterflies flying away for all of them, nodding their heads like yeah. Kiki jammed behind her table. The blonde with the killer voice, who worked at the veterinary clinic I brought clients to sometimes, and her professor beau got down at the edge of the dance floor, beaming at each other and laughing. I felt weirdly jealous of both of them, their ease with each other, with their own bodies. The joy that was palpable between them.

It was almost as embarrassing, somehow, sitting in the dark corner of the bar by myself as it had been when I'd been standing up there singing Johnny Cash. But I couldn't make my feet get up and join the dance floor. Even as Kai waved a hand at me, beckoning me to do just that. Even as Kai fucking *winked* at me. Which made me feel like this wasn't merely a fever dream; I'd actually entered some bizarre alternate universe. But I just...couldn't.

Kai dropped his hand, shook his head at me. Still smiling, he turned his attention to a guy who *was* winking back. Who was slinking around the dance floor, weaving closer and closer to Kai with each hip shimmy. He was wearing a too-tight t-shirt, which, come on; he knew there was a blizzard outside, right? Maybe he was good looking. I didn't know. It was hard to tell at Moonie's, sometimes, who was a creep and who was awesome. There was this dangerous, queer edge to this bar, where it felt like things could implode into a fantasy or a disaster at any moment. Which was why I loved it, of course.

But it was *my* weird escape. Not Kai's. He didn't fit here.

Except, according to the dance floor, he did.

And Kai was...Kai was smiling back at the maybe-hot/maybe-a-hot-mess guy. They circled around each other as Kai sang, came dangerously close to touching.

And wow, I hated it.

My jealousy had a bitter taste in my mouth, like it knew it was illogical but was fully ready to poison me anyway. And that cemented it. This had been a fun experiment and all, reigniting an old, hopeless crush for absolutely no reason.

But I needed to find an exit from this night, and soon.

4

KAI

IT WAS OFFICIAL.

Karaoke was *the best*. All caps: BEST.

I couldn't believe I'd never done it before.

I bounced back to the table, and I knew, somewhere in my brain, that Aiden looked like he wanted to punch something—my face, probably—but I was still too full of adrenaline from the Miley dance party to be overly put out by it this time.

"Well," he said, reaching behind him for his coat before my butt had even hit the seat, "This has been great, but—"

"Wait!" I practically shouted, my smile sliding fast into a frown. "Wait. You can't leave yet. Hold on." I grabbed one of the extra slips of paper and a pencil. "I have to make it up to you, the 'Hurt' thing. I misplayed the game, obviously. I'll do better this round, okay? One more round."

Aiden hesitated, still turned in his seat. He bit his lip, which he always used to do when he was deep into scribbling in his notebooks, truly lost to the outside world. The fact that I had noticed this lip biting, that I remembered it in precise detail, made my new bi-memory smack the inside of my brain and chuckle.

"Come on," I pushed. "You still have most of that beer left."

He let go of his coat. Rather obviously reluctant, but still, he let go of his coat.

"You won't choose a song that people listen to when they're contemplating self-harm?"

"No." I shook my head emphatically. "Promise."

He grumbled, but he reached for a slip of paper, too. "Fine."

More lip biting. And then he wrote something down. I wrote something too, something better, and grabbed both sheets of paper and ran them up to the KJ, whose name I'd learned was Kiki, which was the absolute perfect name for her. I couldn't wait to get to know her better. Miley had inspired confidence in me. I could make Aiden have fun with this night, too; I knew it.

"That guy was flirting with you," Aiden burst out when I sat back down, surprising me once again. Maybe I should keep leaving the table, keep seeing what he'd say next, each time I returned. "During your song. You were flirting back."

I nodded, slowly.

"You shouldn't do that." He frowned. "It's not nice."

"Ah." I took a sip of my soda, cleared my throat, the Miley adrenaline replaced with that now-familiar *here we go* feeling roiling through my gut. I'd learned it was best to get it out of my mouth quickly, whenever an opportunity presented itself, before I lost my nerve. "I guess I should tell you. I'm bi."

Aiden froze, like a deer caught in headlights. It was cute, this look on his face, but I was also surprisingly uncomfortable. I worried, suddenly, that this admission would somehow make Aiden mad. One more reason for McCarstle to hate me, even though I knew that wasn't a rational fear. But maybe he wouldn't believe me, think I was playing him. Or...I didn't know. I was still relatively new at this.

"So," he said, forehead bunched in confusion, "You're not with Mei anymore?"

At this, I laughed, my nerves soothing a little.

"No. Mei and I broke up before graduation, Aiden. Pretty sure she's been engaged to her college boyfriend for like a year. Although," I added, "I could still be bi even if I was still with her."

"I know," Aiden said quickly, covering his face with his hands for a second. "I know. Oh my god. I can't believe Kai Andrews is mansplaining queerness to me."

I laughed.

"You kind of asked for it."

"I know. I'm just...processing. Were you always—"

"No," I said. "I wasn't closeted in high school or anything. Or, well, maybe I was, to myself." I played absently with one of the golf pencils. "For the record, I do not recommend discovering you're bisexual while living in Klamath Falls."

Aiden winced.

"Yeah. That sounds...bleak."

I nodded solemnly. "That's a good way to put it, yeah."

"So are you seeing anyone now?"

Aiden's face flushed after he said this, and he quickly sat back in his chair, fidgeting with his phone. Like he hadn't meant to say it, and it had just slipped out somehow.

"I mean," he said, "Not that it's any of my business."

I stared at him for a minute.

Interesting.

"No," I answered. "Are you? You never really dated anyone back in high school, from what I can remember."

"No," he shook his head. "I mean, I *have* dated people. I'm not a total loser. But I—" He wrapped his hands around his beer. "No."

"I don't think you're a loser," I said. "I never did. You know that, right?"

His eyes flicked to mine, one quick, lightning bolt glance.

"Let's not talk about high school," he said, staring out the window.

"All right." I shrugged. And thought a bit more about what he'd said. "Although you know, I just have to say, I don't think dating history has anything to do with being a loser or not."

He leaned forward, covering his face with his hands again, keeping them there this time.

"Ugh," he mumbled through his fingers. "*Fine*, Mr. Magnanimous. You are right. We are all wonderful rainbows."

I wanted to pry his fingers away from his face. And then kiss him, maybe.

Instead, I laughed, in sort of a helpless way. And then I just fucking asked it.

"Why do you hate me so much?"

Aiden froze again. Peeked at me through his fingers.

He dropped his hands and leaned back in his chair.

"I..." He looked down at his palms. "I don't."

And then Kiki called his name again.

5

AIDEN

I FELT RATTLED as I took the mic once more from Kiki.

Why do you hate me so much?

I guess I should tell you. I'm bi.

There weren't enough people at Moonie's tonight. Kiki was cycling through our songs too fast; I wasn't ready to be back up here again. I didn't want people looking at me, didn't want *Kai* looking at me under these bright ass lights. It felt like he'd already looked at me too much tonight.

I had whiplash from all the different things pinging around in my brain, all the different things I'd felt in...what? The hour, less? That I'd been hanging out with Kai Andrews. I was probably being an asshole to him, and I didn't want to be. I wanted to be like the blonde woman in the purple polka dotted dress. I wanted to be the badass bartender who didn't give a fuck. I wanted to be Kai, singing Miley, getting everyone to their feet. I wanted—

Oh. I didn't have time to think about everything else I wanted, because "I Knew You Were Trouble" was on the screen. And I had about five seconds until I'd have to open my mouth and sing.

Kai had given me Taylor Swift.

Did he...did he know? That I had always secretly been a Swiftie? Was this a gift? Because now I felt kind of bad, about the next song I'd chosen for him. I—

Damn, okay, here came the lyrics. And—oh god, I loved this song.

Still trying that hard to not have fun, McCarstle?

This was my chance, then. To stop being what Kai Andrews thought I was. To stop retreating back into my high school self just because I was suddenly confronted with my high school nemesis/crush. Who was apparently bi now. Whatever. Time to prove I was an adult. By...singing the shit out of Taylor Swift.

And I did. I *did*.

Fun Dress woman, her professor with the skirt, they got to the dance floor first. Kiki came out from behind her KJ station, shook her hips at me. With me? No, I still didn't really know how to shake my hips. But I was moving, a little. I was having fun, dammit.

This song was a fucking *jam*.

I let myself glance at Kai once. He hadn't moved from the table, but I wasn't bothered that he wasn't on the dance floor. It almost felt...respectful, like he was letting me have my moment. But that was probably me projecting. He was smiling, though. I could tell, even from up here, even though he had his fist over his mouth. Like he was trying to hold in an even bigger smile from escaping.

I liked that. I liked being the focus of Kai Andrews's smiles. Maybe that was why I was so angry at him all the time in high school, not just because he was so perfect and so different from me. But because his smiles were always directed at other people. And I wanted them all for me. As illogical, as selfish as that was. And maybe it was only happenstance, that I was alone with him at this bar tonight, that he happened to be smiling at me now.

But he was right. Like he was right about everything. I had spent an inordinate amount of time in my life holding myself back from things. Although, in my own defense, I didn't always see it like that. I wasn't holding myself back from the world; I was simply better at standing in the shadows and observing it. I was *good* at it, observing the world. Writing it down.

It wasn't *sad*, or this tragic way of being; it was just...different. I always liked coming to Moonie's and sitting in the back with Penelope, listening to everyone else sing all their favorite songs, off-key and enthusiastic. It didn't matter that I didn't normally pick up the mic myself. I could still feel it. I still showed up. I was still a part of it, in my own way.

And yet.

Maybe I should take advantage of opportunities when they were presented to me. Like gorgeous men's smiles. To accept the invitation to the dance floor, to put down the pen, to step out of the comfortable shadows. If only just for a little while.

I didn't know what to do with my own smile, though, when the song finally finished and I returned to the table. It was embarrassing, but I couldn't quite keep it off my face. And I apparently wasn't quite brave enough yet, to throw it directly at Kai. Like he had done for me.

"That was a better choice, then," he said. And even though I couldn't make eye contact right then, I could *hear* the smile in his voice, and that was somehow worse than seeing it.

"Yes," I answered. "I, uh. I love Taylor."

Kai chuckled, and it was low and rumbly and extremely pleasing to my core.

"Good," he said.

And before I even had the chance to fully regain my breath, Kiki said Kai's name again.

"Oh," I said quickly. "Kai. Uh."

I had made him promise to not choose any more sad sack songs for me. But I hadn't made that promise in return, for him.

He looked at me as he stood, raising an eyebrow again.

Shit.

"I'm sorry," I said, biting my lip. "In advance."

6

KAI

I blew out a breath as I stared at the screen.

Well. This wasn't fair.

But then again, I'd given Aiden "Hurt." Maybe this was completely fair.

From the corner of my eye, I saw the blonde woman in the bright dress—Lily—stand from their table, reach for her jacket. The idea popped into my head, and I had approximately ten seconds to pull it off.

I rushed to the table and whispered my plea. Lily hesitated, looked over at her partner. They nodded at her with a little smile. She turned, squeezed my shoulder, and walked up to get the second mic from Kiki.

Thank god.

So when I had to start singing about secret chords and David pleasing the Lord, about minor falls and major lifts, at least I wasn't alone. Her voice next to me was gentle and strong, and I focused on her kind face as we made it through the verses. I had learned, over the last few years, that it often was strangers who made the best saviors.

To be clear, I loved "Hallelujah." There probably

wasn't a soul alive who wasn't moved by Jeff Buckley's singular voice. I loved "Hurt," too. Sad men covering sad men. I hadn't been completely trying to make fun of Aiden, although it occurred to me, of course, once he had started singing and scowling through it, that he probably thought that was my sole intent. But just like this one, "Hurt" was a beautiful song. And Aiden deserved beautiful songs.

Although, yeah, probably not necessarily in karaoke form.

I hoped I was making it up to him now, even if I'd grabbed assistance to do it. It was weird, adjusting to this melodic lament after Aiden had just rocked so hard to "I Knew You Were Trouble"—which, damn, had been an amazing thing to witness—he was *so, so* close to smiling at me, I could tell—but Lily and her wonderful voice helped me get there. And soon, I didn't feel awkward at all, standing in the middle of this half-empty, run-down bar in my hometown and singing this sad, sad song. I only felt...every little bit of it.

When it was over, and we handed back our mics, Lily walked over to her partner. Who had been leaning against a wall near the door, watching intently the whole time. They handed her her coat, and wrapped their arms around her shoulders. They kissed her forehead. And then they both turned and left.

And I just stood there, at the corner of the dance floor, watching this small, tender moment.

And I suddenly missed my mom so much it took my breath away.

I turned, walked toward the opposite corner of the room, away from our table. I thought I'd seen a door back here, by the restrooms—yes, there it was. A crooked arrow was hand drawn on a piece of notebook paper, taped to the wall. *PATIO*.

The icy air hit my face as soon as I stepped outside, a welcome shock. I walked to the edge of the small wooden platform, past the picnic tables with frozen ashtrays, their heaps of ash and cigarette butts dusted with snow. It was a covered patio, but the powdery flurries and harsh wind blew through anyway. I stood at its furthest edge, staring out into the distance.

The snow was sticking now, probably had been for some time. There was really nothing else out here. What a funny place for Penelope and Aiden to hang out. I stared at the snow stacking up on a vast lot full of construction vehicles behind the bar, behind a barbed-wire fence, their industrial forms like robotic ghosts.

We should go home soon.

I took a slow, deep breath, the cold almost painful in my lungs.

This moment didn't make much sense. "Hallelujah" had nothing to do with my mom. Although she had always loved music, hummed random snippets of random things all the way until the end.

I had started kissing her on the forehead like that, though. Like Lily's professor had kissed her, before they walked into the night.

Leaning over the hospital bed. Resting my mouth on her forehead for just a moment. It felt like a safe way to say I was sorry, that I wasn't there enough, that this was happening at all. Both of our eyes closed, my touch focused on one part of her that hadn't been worn away, that still felt warm and soft and good. Squeezing her hand, feeling how frail it had gotten, always felt so much scarier.

It wasn't ideal, that this was hitting me now, here, but I'd learned grief never was ideal. Never did make much sense. It hit you when you least expected it, but when you most expected it, too. It was always sort of there. You just didn't have control over when it got loud.

But when it did, I'd decided to hear it. And right now that meant getting some air, even if it was fucking freezing, and simply waiting for it to eventually turn back into a whisper.

The door creaked open behind me, slammed shut.

"Hey."

I glanced back once, to see Aiden lean against the wall next to the door, cross his arms over his chest. He pulled his sweater up over his hands, shivered.

"Hey." I stared back into the snowy wasteland. "Sorry. Just needed a minute."

"Yeah, of course. It's fine."

And then he only stood there. Giving me space. Letting me be quiet.

It was nice, actually. Which was a little surprising. He had definitely wanted to hit me, or bolt, or something, when I first walked into this bar. But I had this gut instinct, right then, that Aiden McCarstle would stand out on this dark, dilapidated patio with me in the snow for an hour, if I wanted him to.

And I found I wanted him to. Or at least, I didn't mind. I was feeling kind of confused, in general, about Aiden McCarstle. But it felt okay that he was out here.

My shoulders drooped. My breath was a white cloud in front of me.

"She went so fast," I said eventually. "We knew the diagnosis wasn't good, but I still didn't expect her to be gone so fast. I think maybe that's why it feels like it's still happening, sometimes. Like my brain's still catching up."

I looked down at the splintered boards under my feet.

"I wish I had moved back before she died. But I didn't.

And now I'm just...here, and she's not. I've been wanting to come back home for forever and now that I'm here, I just feel...off. Like maybe I don't fit here anymore."

Aiden took a long breath behind me.

"That sounds really hard, Kai."

"Yeah." I kicked at a patch of ice. "Sorry. The song just...got to me."

"Understandable," Aiden said. A pause. "I'm sorry."

"Don't be."

"I think...I think you fit here, though. It probably feels different, being here now. But that's all it is. Different. Not wrong."

I wiped my knuckles against my eyes.

"Yeah."

We stood in silence a few minutes longer. I blinked, a lot, and made some kind of weird noises, between my chest and my nose, until I was sure the tears were at bay.

And then I squared my shoulders and turned, finally walking toward him, where he still stood under the one spotlight attached to the outside of the building, shining weak and yellowish onto the dark patio.

He straightened as I approached, stuffing his hands in his pockets.

"We should head out," I said. "It's starting to stick out there."

Aiden swallowed. I watched the bob of his Adam's apple, half of his face in shadow.

"Probably, we should," he said, slowly, like he wasn't one hundred percent certain of what he was about to say. "But...I have one more proposition."

Now, I knew, I knew, that Aiden McCarstle likely did not mean *that* kind of proposition. But something about when he said it this time—maybe it was the fact that I had just gotten overly honest, and he had been kind of nice about it. And the fact that we were the only ones out here, and even though everything around us was pretty objectively ugly, it also felt a little bit holy, with the snow and the silence and the shadows. Or the fact that we were simply probably standing too close, and the wind was blowing one of his curls over his forehead, and he looked so cold that it felt vulnerable, like he wanted me to wrap my arms around him to keep him comfortable. Or I just wanted to do that.

Whatever the reason, something felt charged between us. Like something had shifted. Something brought in on the dry, icy wind. Something that begged for warmth.

"One more round," Aiden said. "We still pick each other's song, but...we pick something we know the other one loves. No more of..." He waved a hand. "Whatever this was. Just our favorite songs."

I studied him. I still felt a little fragile, wanted to make sure he wasn't fucking with me. I didn't think he would, especially after this, out here. But still.

"You think you know one of my favorite songs?"

He nodded, quick, sure.

"Yes." And then, "If you can't think of one for me, it's okay; I can—"

"No," I said. "I got one."

"Oh," he said, a little surprised. "Okay. Then, yeah."

He bit his lip.

"All right," I said. "One more round."

7

AIDEN

THE BAR HAD EMPTIED out even more when we stepped back inside. The place felt barely alive at this point, and I almost panicked, worried we'd be shuffled out before I could make it up to Kai, and we'd have to leave with only the memories of this weird, kind of mean game I'd created. Where I'd made him sing a song that made him sad about his dead mom.

"Hey," I said to Kiki. "Can we still put in a couple requests?"

"Yeah," she nodded. "If you want. But I think we're closing up shop here soon, so make it quick."

I hurried back to the table, scribbled Kai's final song on a slip of paper.

"I'll take them to her," Kai said, and he snatched my paper and walked back to Kiki's table. Where he proceeded to talk with her for longer than it should have taken to drop off our last song requests, especially if they were in a hurry to shut the place down. Kiki typed something on the laptop; Kai leaned over the table to look at the screen. He smiled, nodded; she gave him a thumbs up.

What the hell.

We were quieter when he got back to the table. I sucked down the rest of my beer; he sipped on his vodka soda, or whatever he was drinking. Things felt different, more tense between us, but not necessarily in a bad way. Just in a way that made me itch, wanting to find the right words to describe whatever it was that was happening. Maybe we were friends now. I didn't know. Maybe I'd figure it out later, tomorrow, tonight when I got home, whenever I could get a pen in my hand. I often couldn't actually figure something out until I was physically in the act of writing it down. Then, somehow, between my brain and the paper, I found it.

Hollywood got up to sing an Al Green song. I didn't know what Hollywood's actual name was; that was just what everyone called him. He was an old Filipino man who showed up at Moonie's sometimes, always by himself, always in a full three piece suit. He'd stroll in, sing some random oldie, absolutely kill it, and then immediately leave.

And that was why Penelope and I loved Moonie's.

I hoped Hollywood got home safe tonight, in the snow.

And then Kiki said Kai's name.

I exhaled as he got up to the mic. For the first time all night, I felt truly nervous. Maybe he wouldn't be up to the song, after getting down about his mom; maybe—

"Oh, *fuck* yeah," Kai said into the mic as the song came onto the screen.

And he laughed.

His eyes looked so, so happy, the chocolate of his irises shining under the lights, that my chest expanded with this feeling, like maybe I had done the exact right thing for the first time in my entire life.

It was called "Mr. Blue Sky" by ELO. The Electric

Light Orchestra. And when it started, it didn't matter that there were only three other people left in this bar. Kai performed it like he was looking for an Oscar nomination. Or maybe, more accurately, a Tony. He used the entirety of the dance floor, kicking his feet around, pumping his shoulders up and down in rhythm with the steady, persistent percussion. He spread his arms out at one point and swooped around Moonie's like he was a bird about to take flight. A really buff bird, in a lavender colored sweatshirt, singing about...well, I had no idea what this song was about. It was a strange song.

During a brief break between a verse and a chorus, Kai pointed toward the bar and grinned. I followed his gaze, and to my actual shock, saw the butch bartender nodding her head along with the beat. She rolled her eyes when Kai pointed at her, but it didn't even seem to be in a particularly grumpy way. When the song dived into another verse, as she continued drying off empty pint glasses, she sang along under her breath.

I had never seen her sing along with *anything*.

It took me a second to move my focus back to the dance floor, where Kai was still almost-floating, almost-flying, a glowing island in the middle of this dark, crummy, wonderful little bar.

There was one point where the vocals got kind of robotic and synthesized, and Kai froze, holding his hand over the mic as he sang in an attempt to imitate it, and it was so deeply dorky that I was honestly flabbergasted.

The last minute of the song was only this high-pitched choir making random noises, and Kai just kept bouncing around the dance floor through it, smiling, looking like he was super stoned, until he eventually threw the mic back at Kiki before the last piano notes had tinkled away.

He sprinted back to the table.

"How," he demanded, still grinning. "How did you know?"

I shrugged, suddenly self-conscious.

"It's your pump up song."

And now I was blushing.

"I *know* it's my pump up song!" He hit the table. "But how did *you* know that?"

"Um." I wiped my palms on my jeans. "You gave us a ride, that one time. Me and Pen."

"I did?" he frowned, forehead creasing. I tried to sink further down in my seat, horrified he didn't remember this very important moment in our non-relationship, when I so clearly did.

"Yeah. It was before one of your games. So…"

I used to give Penelope a ride home back in the day, on the rare occasion she didn't have some activity after school, French Club or GSA or running tech for the school plays. And of course, on one of those rare days Junior year, my ancient Volkswagen Jetta wouldn't start. I couldn't remember now, what had even been wrong with it, if it had been the battery, or the starter, or a flat tire. There was always something wrong with it; every cent of my paychecks from the dog boarding kennel I worked at part-time during high school went back into that piece-of-shit car. But it was my one piece of freedom, that car. So I loved it like a child.

What I *do* remember from that day is the moment Penelope's eyes lit up as she saw Kai walk into the student lot. Before I could stop her, she was waving both arms at him.

"Kai'll give us a ride, I bet," she said.

And I had to turn, and watch him wave back, and walk toward us in his soccer uniform, the laces of his cleats tied and slung around his neck. Those soccer shorts always seemed an *inch* too short, showing just slightly too much of Kai Andrews's sculpted quads for my poor, extremely gay teenaged system.

"I would," he'd said. "But I have a game. Have to be on the pitch in ten. Could give you both a ride home afterward, though?"

No one calls it a pitch here, I thought.

But Penelope had nodded enthusiastically.

"I always mean to get to more of your games anyway! You're not busy, right, Aiden?" And then she'd shoved my shoulder, the traitor. "Let's go watch some futbol!"

Kai had used the five minutes it took to drive from our high school to the soccer field, a few blocks away, to blast "Mr. Blue Sky." His pump up song, he'd called it. And then Penelope and I had watched him play soccer, and it had been a beautiful fall day, and he had scored two goals, and I had been miserably jealous of all his teammates who got to hug him.

He drove us home afterward, as promised, and I sat silently in his back seat, surrounded by the smell of him— sweat, and grass, and glory—and tried to hold it in my lungs for the rest of the night.

"Huh," Kai sat back in his chair now, took a last sip of his gin and tonic or whatever it was. "That makes sense then. God, I haven't listened to that song in forever."

He flicked his eyes to mine, and they looked darker and sparklier all at once, somehow, than they had all night. Like stars in a midnight sky.

"Thanks for that, Aiden."

"And it looks like this next one will be our last song of the night, folks," Kiki shouted, and I jumped. "Aiden, get back up here! Everyone else, make sure you get home safely tonight!"

I clutched the mic to my chest after Kiki handed it to

me, blinking as I turned to face the screen. A bittersweet feeling was fizzling through my veins. This night had been weird as hell, but...well, I was kind of sad to see it end. I wasn't one hundred percent positive, but I was pretty sure I was glad it had happened.

And then I saw the song on the screen.

I stopped blinking. Simply stared.

Oh...my god.

I hardly had time to process before the first frenzied guitar chords smashed into my consciousness. I didn't think they even had this song available as a choice for karaoke. No, I *knew* they didn't have this song; I'd tried looking it up in the binder before, but—

Here it was, on the screen. "Aside" by The Weakerthans.

My favorite fucking song, from when I was in high school.

I didn't have time to even begin to wrap my head around the fact that Kai knew this, a fact that made no sense, being that I had hardly talked to Kai Andrews about anything in high school, and certainly not my favorite song. I had never driven *him* home in my Jetta; he had never sat next to me and listened to these lyrics curl around him like they had always curled around me, sure and snug and true.

God, I barely had to look at the screen. I knew them all by heart.

And in a beat, I was time traveling.

Every line hit me in the chest, just like they always had, but there was this part where John Samson sings about being lonely and unconsoled and then, in the same breath: *I am so much better than I used to be.*

It was so easy, looking back, to be who you were supposed to be in high school. To slip inside a certain mold. To be angry, to be lonely, to be viciously full of feel-ing. I knew what was expected of me: the grades, the quiet, the constant, barely contained, unnameable heartache. Knew it was all just this test I had to get through, and then I'd get out.

It felt easy to hate Kai in high school, to hate him and be a little in love with him all at the same time. Because it didn't matter. It was so easy to believe that nothing mattered, as long as you got through.

And then you graduated, and the real world crashed in.

And it wasn't enough anymore. To simply hide behind your favorite songs, in the shitty poetry you scribbled on every blank surface you could find. The life you'd been waiting to escape into for your entire journey through the public school system was suddenly just *there*. And it turned out you had to...do something with it.

I had spent the last five years of my life trying to do something with it, but never knowing if I was doing it quite right. Maybe not exactly failing, but flailing. Waiting for a clear, understandable path that never appeared. A ship without an anchor.

But on the dance floor of Moonie's, singing along to my favorite song, somewhere around the first chorus I let it all go. My uncertainty about my life choices. Whatever had happened in this bar tonight. Everything else disappeared, and I let myself love the frantic, painful youth of this song again, its relentless joy. And inside its fuzzy guitars and fast drum beats, I let myself love myself a little, too, the Aiden who had loved this song at seventeen, and the Aiden who loved this song still, now.

Because I *was* so much better than I used to be.

Sure, I hated grad school. I hated that I was in grad school at all, that I knew I would hate it but applied anyway, because I hadn't known what else to do. And *attending grad school, pursuing my MFA* was at least a tangible thing I could tell people—my parents, my friends, Kai Andrews—when asked what I was doing with my life.

But I had still lived, these last five years, more than I had let myself back then. I still preferred the shadows, when it came to things like karaoke. I still mostly felt anchorless. But I had grabbed hold of life how I could, in my own ways. I had taken long road trips, up into the Olympic rain forests, down the Pacific Coast Highway, down to Baja California. I had stood underneath the shelter of redwoods. I had felt the ocean cover my toes. I had fallen in love.

It hadn't worked out, in the end, with Niall, but I had still been in love once, something that had felt impossible to me back in high school, and that counted for something. I had had poems published in Tin House, in Ploughshares, in Lambda, in The Iowa Review, and I knew poems weren't exactly the same as building ships with your bare hands, but they meant something to me.

I wasn't a child. I *had* tried to have fun. I had been something, in the brief but long space between now and the last time Kai Andrews knew me. I couldn't explain out loud, exactly, what that something was—only the words in my notebooks could—but a wild part of me, just then, wanted to tell Kai Andrews about some of it, the memories I had managed to make for myself. Or at least try to tell him some of it. Because maybe he would listen. Maybe he would smile, just for me.

Not right now, though. Because this moment, these lyrics and this song and this feeling, were all mine.

Even though it was there, in the periphery of my mind, the whole time.

The knowledge that this moment was one Kai Andrews had given me.

When it was over, I handed the mic back to Kiki and walked to our table, feeling raw and open now that the song was over, unsure what to do next.

But Kai was on top of it. He stood as I came near. Handed me my coat.

"Let's cash out," he said.

At the bar, it felt like we were standing too close.

"Okay," I said when the bartender turned to run Kai's card. "How did *you* know? About that song?"

Kai drummed his fingers on the bar.

"Senior year, we were in pre-calc?"

I nodded. As if I didn't remember sitting next to Kai Andrews, feeling his presence, every damn day of that year.

"You were always writing the lyrics of that song on the cover of your book." He shrugged. "And it was—"

He paused. I turned my body toward his, gave him my full attention.

"It was different, when you wrote the lyrics, than when you wrote your poems. When you wrote poems, you were all—" He scrunched his shoulders up, hid his chin in his chest. "But when you wrote the lyrics you seemed relaxed, like you weren't even thinking about them." He unscrunched. "And there were certain lines you wrote over and over. So I looked them up one day, and found the song."

"And you remembered the name of the song, five years later."

He shot me a quick look, before looking down and signing his receipt.

"You remembered mine," he mumbled. Which was

weird, because Kai wasn't a mumbler. "It's not that hard to believe."

"And you made Kiki look it up?"

He snapped the pen back on the counter, slid the paper toward the bartender.

"Yeah, she said she can look up pretty much any song on YouTube, if it's not already in their system."

"Huh," I said.

"*Huh*," he repeated, in a weird little voice, like he was making fun of me, like we were ten years old.

And then he threw on his coat and walked out of Moonie's.

Quickly, I scribbled my own signature on the line and chased after him.

"Hey."

He stopped, turned. I caught up to him, breathless from the cold air hitting my lungs again. It was snowing even harder now, already resting on Kai's brown hair, brushing down the tip of his nose. The entire parking lot was covered in white, and it all seemed shockingly bright after the darkness of the bar, the night lit up by the harsh floodlights of the lot, the flurries above Kai's head high-lighted in the glow. The lot was practically abandoned, waiting only for Kiki, the bartender, the last lonely souls of Moonie's. It felt like we were all alone again, in this strange, pretty plain of concrete and snow.

He was wearing this nice grey peacoat, and it looked both funny and perfect on top of his purple hoodie. And I knew, with certainty, that if I didn't do this now, I never would. So I reached out with both hands and grabbed those lapels. They were warm and scratchy on my fingers, and I pulled, but Kai was already pushing toward me, my efforts for naught. I had barely angled my chin toward his when his own hands reached up, gripped the back of my neck, so rough and strong, and I had imagined the feel of those hands, just like that, so many times, that I think I may have let out an embarrassing little sigh before our lips even met.

And when they did, it was all open mouths and tongues from the start, like we were both hungry.

God, it was so good.

His mouth was so hot, the skin of his chin so warm and prickly, this blazing kiss caught in the midst of the blizzard around us. The unexpected heat of it stole my breath, my inhibition, my ability to feel anything but *him*, no longer the boy with the mouthwatering thighs and erotic knuckles, but a full-blown *man*, who built ships and felt things and knew all the words to "Party in the USA."

Who still knew my favorite song.

A swell of emotion caught me in the throat like a right hook, and I was seized with a kind of terror, that the kiss would end, and the magic of the snow and the songs and the night would be over, when I had just figured out that I needed it. And even though I could literally barely breathe, and needed to break the kiss, I found myself pressing into him more, harder, so that he stumbled. I moved my hands to wrap around his back and pull him close, as close as possible, so he wouldn't leave, and this wouldn't be done.

But eventually, of course, Kai tore his mouth away from mine, on this kind of guttural moan that almost broke me.

"Fuck," I breathed, leaning my forehead against his, gasping the freezing air back into my lungs. "Fuck."

Kai didn't say anything, only stood there with his hands still in my hair, catching his breath with me.

"I have a proposition now," he said at length, nudging his nose against mine, each word a gust of warm breath on my skin. "Come home with me, Aiden."

I wanted to swoon against him, like a half-dressed lady on an old school romance cover.

Instead I merely stood, frozen.

"I live nearby," he said when I didn't respond. "We can take the bus. You shouldn't drive home anyway, in this. Did you drive?"

I nodded, barely, my skin brushing against his.

"Okay then. Come on." He stepped away, tugged at my hand.

I let myself be led to the bus stop right in front of Moonie's. Let my hand slip inside Kai's. Let myself be pulled to Kai's chest, his arms wrapped around me now, rubbing circles on my back, keeping me warm. I felt his nose sink into my hair, felt more than heard his sigh.

I closed my eyes and counted to ten. Made myself be very quiet.

I always felt more grounded, when things were quiet. And with each minute that the cold air seeped in, with each minute we lived further and further away from Moonie's and the temporary magic of our favorite songs, I began to finally freak out.

A song, really, is nothing but a fantasy. Real life wasn't lived in chords and pretty melodies.

I couldn't quite imagine myself, anymore, telling Kai about the time I went to Baja. About Tin House and Ploughshares.

I could imagine myself kissing him again, of course. And whatever else was going to happen next. I could imagine doing many things with Kai Andrews, being that I'd already imagined them.

Fuck, that kiss. I shivered in Kai's arms, and he squeezed me tighter. That kiss was going to be seared into my memory for the rest of my life.

But if anything, we knew each other even less now than

we had back then, were even more of strangers to each other. What right did I have to want to comfort him about his mom? None. I had no right to want any piece of him. And I could still barely fathom what Kai thought of me, what he had ever thought of me, why he didn't walk right back out of Moonie's tonight when we learned Penelope wouldn't be coming.

But whatever picture he had of me, it wasn't accurate. It wasn't accurate, because I didn't even know what an accurate picture of me was. I was better than I used to be, and maybe for a few moments back there I had felt okay, but I was still a mess.

We still didn't fit, Kai Andrews and me. I had fit with Niall. But this...this didn't make sense. There was a reason Kai had only ever been a fantasy for me, back in high school.

Best to understand, now, if we were going to do this, what was actually happening here. In some funny twist of fate—otherwise known as Penelope Vossey—Kai and I had met again tonight. We had gotten caught up in some dangerous mixture of nostalgia and alcohol. And now we were possibly going to fuck, and it was probably going to be good.

And then we'd wake up and go back to our lives. Obviously. Our very different, unconnected lives. And it would be...fine. If anything, I should be grateful this was happening at all. How often did we actually get to live out high school fantasies? Maybe I'd been good this year after all. Maybe this was the best gift Santa had ever brought me.

I just had to be careful. Because part of me already felt a little hollow as the feelings I'd felt inside Moonie's faded. How vulnerable it had been, singing in front of each other, the horrible song choices and the good ones. How he'd let me witness a little bit of his mourning, out on the patio. The way my stomach churned every time he smiled, and when he'd been so fucking happy during "Mr. Blue Sky." Parts of it already felt far away somehow, a memory, something I was already over-romanticizing in my head.

Kai's lips grazed my jaw. His tongue pressed down the side of my neck, and *nnrrrgghhh*, that felt good. I stopped hiding my face in his shoulder, stopped this mental spiral. I shoved him back against the plastic wall of the bus shelter, took his face in my hands and smashed our mouths together again. Felt the slide of his tongue against mine again. This was carnal, and there was absolutely nothing nonsensical about that. Grab hold of opportunities when they presented themselves, right? I wanted this man. I could let myself have him, for a night.

If I was careful.

He released another low moan, reverberating against my lips. Kai was vocal, apparently, and it was going to drive me out of my mind. He grabbed my hips, pulled me flush against him. It was honestly a bit uncomfortable, the hot urgency of our bodies clashing against the cold night, my pants too tight for this. I needed to get inside somewhere, anywhere, needed to get through all these layers of distracting clothing, needed to just *touch* him and then I'd be able to lose myself again, like how it had been during the songs, able to forget how perfect he still was, how much it hurt to even let myself imagine a future where we weren't totally incongruous. Where a person like him could be mine.

He broke away again when we needed to breathe.

"McCarstle," he rumbled, shaking his head. "Who fucking knew."

He reached a hand around and squeezed my ass, and I yelped a little. My brain was apparently acquainted enough with his mouth at this point—soft, hot, aggressive but not too sloppy, absolutely acceptable—but Kai Andrews squeezing my ass was still a shock to the system.

"Andrews," I said, truth spilling out. "God, I want you in all the ways."

Kai's lips parted, and he stared at me. It was darker here at the bus stop, outside of the glow of the floodlights in the Moonie's parking lot, but I thought I could see the heat flare in his eyes anyway. Approval. Desire. For *me*.

Teenage Aiden had come at least twice already. Electrified in my subconscious, constantly whispering *holy shit* in my ear.

Sex. That was all this was.

It was already feeling easier to convince myself. That this was a fine idea.

Because sex was incredible.

I moved in again, ready to suck on his lips some more, or maybe his neck, or—

A loud, crunching noise behind me made me jump back, my heart thrumming in my ears.

The bus sighed as it opened its doors. I squinted at the bright lights of the interior. Shit.

I fumbled in my pocket for my phone, my fingers cold and slow, my eyes blurry as I tried to find the right app. I'm sure the driver had seen worse, picking up people from the Moonie's stop in the middle of the night on a Saturday, but I still felt slightly mortified.

"Sorry," I said to the driver, who looked bored and probably did not care that I was sporting a ridiculous hardon, just that I was slowing down his route. In the snow. "Sorry, sorry."

Finally, I found the app, and hallelujah, I had a few bucks on it. I heard a strange muffled noise behind me, and looked back as I swiped my phone on the reader.

Kai was laughing at me.

This asshole.

I scowled.

As soon as we were alone again, I was going to use teeth this time.

8

KAI

AIDEN PRACTICALLY RAN to the back of the bus. I followed more slowly, trying to calm both my erection and the goofy smile on my face, as the different shades of Aiden McCarstle tumbled through my head.

I was fascinated by the Aiden who had been so clearly happy on the dance floor for that last song, this Aiden I'd never been allowed to see before, open and real. I was turned on as hell by the Aiden who grabbed hold of my coat and pushed me against the bus shelter, who kissed me with such focused, unabashed passion.

I had wanted to kiss him so badly, all night really, and especially after our last songs. But I didn't know if I had the courage to make the move myself. I had never had the courage, really, to make moves; almost all of my previous relationships were usually initiated by the other party, and I was even more nervous around men. Still felt too new and insecure at this to show what I wanted. But the moment Aiden reached for me, it was like he granted me permission, and it had felt so freeing, and so...hot. And beautiful, somehow, underneath the falling snow.

But I could tell, as soon as the squelch of the bus had broken Aiden out of our make out reverie, that he was feeling antsy again. He crossed his arms over his chest and stared resolutely out the window as I sat next to him on the back row of seats.

And this Aiden, this Aiden who almost dropped his phone at least five times trying to bring up the public transit app, who was bouncing his knee next to me as the bus rumbled away from the stop, who had scowled at me across the table back at Moonie's—this Aiden, I knew.

And god help me, but I could fully admit it now.

I adored this Aiden.

I remembered this time back in high school, when I stepped out into the hall one morning and Aiden was there. His backpack had split wide open, and all of this stuff had fallen everywhere. It was almost comical, like he was playing a caricature of a teenage klutz in a TV show, the way he was frantically trying to shove everything back into his bag. And there was just so *much* of it, so many disorganized papers and half falling apart notebooks. He'd been so flustered, so pissed, that he'd barely been able to look at me as I'd helped him. I mean, he barely looked at me, in general, but it seemed more pointed that time.

I'd spent the rest of the day thinking about it—the flush of his cheeks, all those wrinkled papers—and smiling to myself.

I rested my elbows on my knees now, steepled my fingers loosely in front of me. Looked over, watched Aiden's jaw click back and forth as he kept staring out at the snowy night.

I didn't know if I could pinpoint it, exactly, what it was about Aiden McCarstle that made me feel a little giddy inside. It was this kind of restless, irrepressible energy, this quiet intensity. Like he was constantly buzzing inside, like he couldn't keep all of his feelings inside his skin. It was why he was always hunching over, sinking down into his seat, bouncing his knee like he was now. Like if he let himself stand fully, actually stretch out his spine and let it all out, he'd explode.

I placed a hand on his knee, and he stilled. Finally moved his gaze from the window down to my knuckles.

I caressed his knee over his jeans with my thumb, once, twice.

And because I couldn't help myself, because he'd given me permission in the parking lot to be bold, I dropped my head to his neck, darting out my tongue to the tender skin there. I moved closer, shoving my leg against his.

"Kai," he said, voice low, a little annoyed, a lot sexy. "They have cameras on here."

Involuntarily, I let out a snort. Moving my head, I looked around the bus. I'd normally be anxious about this kind of thing, too, but there was exactly one other passenger, up at the very front.

"Aiden. Do you think the bus driver is going to call security on me—in the middle of a snowstorm—for getting you hard?"

Aiden closed his eyes, let out a slow, dramatic breath.

"I hate you."

I looked down at the bulge in his pants.

"Doesn't look like you do."

But I moved my hand away from his leg. Shifted back to my seat, leaving a few safe inches between us again. And looked out the opposite window, grinning to myself.

"How much further until your stop?"

I tried to deduce where we were. The bus had its snow chains on; we were moving through the seemingly abandoned city at a glacial pace.

"Only a few more. Five, ten minutes."

"Okay."

I glanced back over at him. He kept his legs still now, his eyes closed, like he was meditating. Angry meditating. Until I reached over him to grab the cord for my stop. At which point his eyes popped open and he looked down at my arm, stretched over his chest, and sucked in a small breath. I caught his gaze, held it for a moment, before lowering my hand back to my lap. His cheeks were pink from the cold, his lips a tad puffier, redder, from our kisses.

I want you in all the ways.

Same, McCarstle. God. Fucking same.

We departed the bus, barreled through the snow for the block and a half it took to walk to my building—the wind had really picked up—and walked through the parking lot to the elevator in silence. I swiped my card and hit the button, my insides fizzy with nerves.

My building was less than a year old, one of those new steel-and-glass monstrosities of the inner East Side that was, according to most people, ruining the city. Taller than anything else around it, sparkling and out of place. I lived in the epitome of gentrification. And it only occurred to me now, as we rode the elevator toward my floor, that Aiden would absolutely hate it.

Aiden probably lived in some gorgeous, rambling Craftsman further out on the East Side. I imagined him sharing the house with other artists, other poets. Painters, illustrators, people who read essays and graphic novels. It was probably full of plants and natural light, worn floor-boards, someone always baking something delicious while someone else played an acoustic guitar. Dried herbs hanging in the kitchen window. All of the furniture from vintage thrift stores, bright and quirky and homey. Maybe they owned chickens.

The truth was, I wanted my own falling apart house

someday, out in the country. Close enough to the city so that I could still easily visit, far enough away that I could own a decent plot of land. Where I could spend my days fixing up the property, adopting dogs and letting them roam free. Where I could grow a garden worthy of a spread in the *Sunset* magazine my mom always subscribed to. Where I could sit on a porch, watch the clouds drift over Mt. Hood. Wake to quiet sunrises.

But when I'd moved back here a couple months ago, something about the sharp, clean lines of these shiny new apartment buildings appealed to me. They were the opposite of the house I'd grown up in, the opposite of all the memories that still awaited me, looming, in that house. I wanted something new, to make this move home feel different, so I knew I wasn't moving backward.

And...I didn't want to be alone. My place down in Klamath Falls had been pretty isolated. I thought maybe living in a place like this, where I could hear neighbors banging around behind their own walls, where I could smile at them in the mailroom, would make me feel a little less alone.

When I'd toured this one, and seen the view from this floor—the city below, and then expanding clear across the river, to the foothills beyond—it'd clinched it. I had felt safe. At peace.

At work, I spent so much time trapped in dark, hot, dangerous places, confined by my heavy protective gear. And I loved it, most of the time; it was its own sort of peace. But whenever I came back here, walked in and saw the view, I felt light and free again.

Aiden walked over to that view as soon as we walked inside the apartment.

I tossed my keys on the kitchen counter, put my coat on the hook.

Cautiously, I walked toward him, leaned against the back of my couch behind him. Looked at the planes of his shoulder blades as he stared out the window. I wanted to reach my arms around him, slide my hands under that frayed sweater, kiss the back of his neck.

But the air between us felt fragile, now that we were here, and I didn't want to do the wrong thing. I'd lost the taunting confidence I had on the bus. I wanted him to take charge again, the way he'd pushed against me in the Moonie's parking lot. To turn and knock me down onto the couch, or command me to strip, or grab my sweatshirt and twirl me around, kiss me against the glass.

"It's a nice view, actually," he said eventually. I smiled a little. The *actually* gave him away. He did hate it.

Finally, he turned.

"Are we just drunk?"

My stomach sank. Oh god. He hated my apartment, and he hated me, just like I'd always thought. He was going to leave.

I shook my head.

"I...don't drink. I was drinking Sprite at the bar."

His eyes widened.

"You were drinking *Sprite?* Oh my god." He covered his face with his hands again. "Of course you don't drink. Alcohol would ruin your perfect specimen of a body. You probably don't eat carbs, either."

I laughed a half-laugh.

"No, no, it's just...alcohol doesn't settle well with me, I've learned. That's all."

"*Sprite,*" he repeated after a minute, shaking his head. "That's so..." He dropped his hands. "Fucking cute."

And then he was on me, and I actually did almost fall back onto the couch, but he caught me, his hands digging into my biceps. His tongue clashed against mine again, that intensity he'd hit me with at Moonie's resurrected, his hands moving to slip under my sweatshirt and the t-shirt underneath.

"Off," he tore his mouth away to say, tugging at my sweatshirt. "Take these off."

My skin buzzed at the command, and I complied immediately, throwing both t-shirt and sweatshirt onto the couch behind me. Aiden ran his hands over my shoulders, down my chest, rested them on my stomach, his eyes following the path of those hands as they traveled. His fingers were long, slender and cold. I put my hands over his, still resting on my stomach, to warm them.

"Jesus," he said.

And then he leaned in, and *bit* my neck where it met my shoulder, like a fucking vampire.

I gasped in surprise and pain. And moaned when he ran his tongue over the point of impact.

"Sorry," he murmured into my sternum.

"I liked it." It surprised me, but I really had. And now I tugged at his sweater. "Your turn."

His sweater and black t-shirt underneath joined mine on the couch, and I studied his pale, narrow frame, the jut of his collarbones, everything about his body as sharp and precise as his face, just as I had imagined it. Taut. Powerful, in his own way.

I reached around him, scratched my fingers up his back, brought him back to me. Kissed him again. And as our mouths danced, my hands drifted downward, fumbled with the button, the zipper of his jeans. I felt almost frantic now, feeling his skin against mine, like I needed to touch him immediately, make sure he didn't get away. And so I did, reaching inside those jeans as soon as I found the room, grasping him over his briefs.

His breath stuttered, his mouth pulling away from mine.

He groaned softly, a light exhalation against my cheek.

"I can't believe this is happening," he said, staring down at my hand. "I've dreamed about this for so long."

I paused.

"You have?"

His eyes flicked to mine for just a second, face flushing, and I wondered if he'd actually meant to say that out loud.

"Well," he gestured with an impatient hand toward my chest. "I mean. You know what you look like."

I grinned.

"You think I'm hot?"

Aiden only sighed through his nose, clenching his jaw. After a second, he gritted out, "Yes."

And then he kissed me again, most likely to shut me up, but I couldn't stop smiling. He grunted his displeasure into my lips.

But this was a revelation to me.

I pushed him back with a hand on his chest.

"Okay, wait," I said, feeling like I was about to burst with glee. "Did you ever jerk off while thinking about me, back in high school?"

Aiden rolled his eyes. "Of course I did. Seriously, this cannot be a surprise to you. Can we just get back to—"

"Oh my god." I pressed my fingers into my temples. "This is absolutely a surprise to me. I thought you hated me, Aiden. Thought I was just some dumb jock."

"Well," he sliced a hand through the air. "Masturbation isn't exactly deep, Kai."

I frowned. The giddy feeling inside me froze immediately, sank like a stone into my gut.

I stood up from the back of the couch, pushing him away.

"So you did think I was a dumb jock. You still probably think I'm a dumb jock. This is…"

I shook my head and stalked into the kitchen.

This was bullshit, was what it was.

It wasn't that I was anti-meaningless sex. Okay, so maybe I never thought sex was completely meaningless, but I didn't need someone to be my soulmate to sleep with them.

I just hadn't known that was what we were doing, here.

I had thought things between us tonight felt different.

Being only a hot body to Aiden McCarstle was about the most demeaning thing I could think of. It made me feel small and slightly nauseous, like I had misinterpreted everything. And I had spent too many years figuring out who I really was, already felt too old, to put up with that.

It also made me not like Aiden McCarstle very much.

And for whatever dumb reason, I still wanted to like Aiden McCarstle.

I grabbed a glass from the cabinet, filled it with water from the sink. My mouth felt too sticky sweet from all that soda. I needed to clear my head.

"Kai." Aiden leaned against my kitchen counter, arms crossed over his bare torso. "Look, sorry. I don't think you're a dumb jock. But…" He sighed again, eyes stormy, staring at some spot near the floor behind me. "Can't we just fuck?"

"No." I crossed my arms too, leaning back against the wall. "I need to know why. *Why* we're about to fuck."

He glared at me, clicking his jaw back and forth. And this time, I didn't think it was cute.

When he didn't say anything, I accidentally exploded.

"You know why I want to fuck *you*, McCarstle?" I pushed away from the wall, pointed at his infuriating face. "Because I think you're brilliant. Because I read every poem you wrote in high school, at least the ones you published, the ones I saw you write in your notebooks in pre-calc."

Aiden froze, face blanching. His jaw dropped open a little.

"But you know what?" I threw my hands in the air. "It's not even that. You could be a brilliant writer; who cares. You could also be an incredible asshole. And I think you've always *tried* to be, at least to me, for some reason. But I know Penelope wouldn't love you so much if you were an asshole. And I don't think the guy I actually had a really good time with tonight was an asshole. It's like…"

I put my hands on my hips, staring past him, trying to explain it to myself as much as to him.

"It's like you only show who you are sometimes. Like you're scared of it. Or maybe you only show it to the people you trust. Which is fine, but you never, ever let me see it in high school. Until tonight, when you did surprising things, like sing karaoke, and…kiss me." I took the briefest of breaks to lick my lips, swallowing, before I kept going. "And when you let yourself go, you're so…bright, and funny, and interesting. And it makes me want to crack you right open, so I can see that all the time. I bet when you fuck, you let yourself be like that. So *that's* why I want to fuck you."

I crossed my arms again and retreated back to my wall. My entire body felt warm, like I was blushing all the way to my toes. I was exhausted, suddenly, and almost wanted McCarstle to just go home at this point. Enough humiliation for one evening.

Aiden, at least, must have been suffering from the same body heat affliction I was, because his face was bright red, even though it was actually pretty cold in here. I should have turned up the thermostat when we came in. He dropped his arms, crossed them again. Opened his mouth, closed it. Looked everywhere but at me.

Until eventually, he closed his eyes. Took a deep breath through his nose. And when he opened his eyes again, they never strayed from my face. He uncrossed his arms and walked toward me, slow but steady, like a predator. I swallowed again, trying not to squirm, until he was so close I could feel the warmth of him, smell his body wash, or cologne, or whatever it was, that I had inhaled when he'd first kissed me—something surprisingly floral, light and clean, like daisies and jasmine, a gulp of spring air after a sudden storm.

He reached a hand out and ran his fingertips over my left shoulder.

"Tell me about these," he said softly.

I looked down at his hand on top of my tattoos. It wasn't what I expected him to say; it was not an apology or an explanation. And I was a little annoyed I was the one who had to keep doing the emotional labor here. But I suppressed my sigh and answered him anyway, like the pushover I was.

"That's my mom," I said, pointing at the *Carol* in cursive script, although I thought he should have been able to guess that. "And her favorite flowers."

Boldly shaped, pastel colored peonies wrapped around my shoulder, interspersed with smaller, crisper purple asters and twining branches of a cherry blossom. They surrounded my mom's name, drifted down to surround the head of a dopey, pure hearted shepherd mix on my bicep.

"And that's Jack."

"Jack?" Aiden raised his eyes from my shoulder to my face.

"It's what they named him at the shelter." I shrugged. "Didn't want to change it, in case he'd gotten used to it."

He smiled a little, the tiniest uplift of the corner of his mouth, and he looked back at my shoulder again.

"Was he your dog when you were a kid?"

I shook my head.

"No, I got him when I moved down south. It was, um." I shifted on my feet. "A little lonely, moving to a brand new place by myself. Jack was pretty much my best friend in Klamath Falls."

Aiden moved his fingertips down the length of my arm. Rubbed his thumb against my wrist.

"He died about six months ago," I added, my mouth seeming to move independently of my brain. I didn't know why I was telling Aiden this, right now.

"I'm sorry," Aiden whispered. And then, moving his hands to my stomach, which made me shiver, "It must have been hard, losing your mom and then Jack."

I looked down at his hands, fluttering around my skin. I was having a little trouble keeping my breathing steady.

"Is that why you want to fuck me? Because I have a dead mom and a dead dog?" I managed to get out. "Because I have to say, that doesn't feel great either."

He shook his head, slowly, as slow as his fingers were moving.

And that was what made me start to crumble, I think. Everything up until now had been fast, hard, hot, wet.

But the tiny circles he was making now—on my stomach, on my shoulders, across my chest—were so slow and gentle. Butterflies whispering up my ribs. It melted me.

"No," he said. "I don't want you because of those things. Thank you for telling me about them, though." He paused, his eyes still focused on my shoulder. "And you were never just a dumb jock to me. I'm sorry for making you think that."

He sighed, but it was quiet, almost helpless sounding.

"Kai, I want you because you're good." He stared at me then, eyes steady and dark. His fingers grazed their way to my chin. "You are so, so good."

I stared back. It shouldn't have surprised me, really. That he could make the world vibrate in one little word. Somehow imbue everything I couldn't with simplicity. I felt it so deeply, somehow, let my chest puff up with pride. And I wanted it so badly. To be good for Aiden McCarstle.

I didn't think about it. Felt myself doing it more than understanding actionable thought. Never breaking eye contact, I slid down the wall, put my hands behind my back. And I waited there, on my knees, for Aiden to tell me what to do next.

9

AIDEN & KAI

HOLY FUCKING SHIT.

I stared down at Kai Andrews, on his knees, for me.

Okay, I did not see this one coming.

I had pictured *myself* on my knees for Kai Andrews, plenty of times before, but this...

I scrunched my fingers into my hair, recalibrating.

I think you're brilliant.

All right, so there was a lot going on in my head, right now, but I could handle this. I could handle Kai and his soft, pretty tattoos on his sculpted body, and all those...things, he had said, and the way my heart was taking flight in my chest, freakishly fast and breath stealing, like a hummingbird.

Yes. This was fine.

I breathed out, nodded to myself, my hands still fisted in my hair. These were all good developments. It could still just be sex; it'd just be *better* sex than I had even anticipated, knowing that Kai was hot and charming *and* sweet, and—

And oh my god. The fucker was laughing at me again.

"Hey," I dropped my hands, frowning. "Hey, you're not supposed to be on your knees and *laughing* at me. That's not how this works."

"Sorry." Kai schooled his features, but barely. His hands were still clenched tightly behind him, but his eyes were glinting, smiling up at me. "Sorry. I'm new at this. You're just really...is this okay? Are you okay?"

I stared down at him, and weirdly, I felt a little bit of Moonie's seep back into my system. How that woman had sung "Hallelujah" with him, how unashamed Kai had been to ask for her help. It had felt like cheating, when I saw him go ask her to sing with him, but as I looked at him on his knees now, it only felt...honest. To ask for what you needed.

"Bedroom," I said, and my voice sounded rough even to my own ears. A little of my own honesty, seeping in. "And take off the rest of your clothes when you get there."

He listened very well.

Not five minutes later, I was in Kai Andrews's bedroom, staring at him laid out on his bed, naked and waiting for me.

It was a nice bed. I focused on this, and not Kai's naked body, because that was still—my brain was still processing that.

His bedroom had the same ridiculous view as the living room. It had surprised me, that Kai lived here, but he had filled the sterile space with nice things, things I imagined him making himself. Like the rough hewn wooden head-board behind him. High school soccer star turned into hunky bisexual lumberjack. I imagined him in Klamath Falls, chopping wood whenever he wasn't welding, crafting classy furniture with his bare hands while Jack slept at his feet.

Or maybe he'd bought it all on Wayfair. What did I know?

Sex. Focus on the sex.

I stripped off my own pants, underwear, socks. Felt him watching me. Crawled onto the bed, crawled over him. I touched the mark on his neck where I'd bitten him earlier. He didn't react, just kept watching me. Waiting.

I sat back on my heels, examined the headboard more closely. It wasn't ideal, all abstract, no good posts or rungs to hang onto. But there was a reading light screwed into one section, a nice industrial touch, the contrast of hard metal against the warm wood. I lifted one of his arms toward it, and he understood, raising his other arm willingly, adjusting himself so he could reach. It was a touch too high, so that he wasn't completely lying down or completely sitting, his neck arched awkwardly, likely a little uncomfortable.

"This okay?" I trailed a hand down his chest. Fuck, it was a good chest.

"Yeah."

"Good."

I leaned back again, settled myself over his thighs. His body looked extra long and graceful with his arms raised above his head like that, if you could consider all those muscles and all that dark hair—under his arms, across his chest, trailing down his stomach—graceful. Which I did.

And while I wanted to do very rough, animalistic things with Kai Andrews, kneeling over him while he was like this—so pretty, so patient, so willing—I still couldn't quite believe he was giving this to me. A gift. It felt exactly like it had when I'd picked up the mic from Kiki and saw that he'd chosen "Aside" for me. Like he was giving me permission to...how had he put it? Crack myself wide open.

I had never fantasized about it happening quite like this. But it happening like this—Kai waiting for my instructions, wanting me to take charge—made me feel calm. Like my brain had never been brave enough to envision it this way, but it immediately felt right. Everything in my universe right then felt palpable and honest—him, me, this room—no longer a surreal dream. He was no longer the unattainable golden boy I could never have. We were just two people.

And I realized it wasn't a gift, actually, him submitting to me. Not exactly. Because it was shared. Like the moment he slid to the floor in the kitchen, we had started an intimate conversation. Like wordlessly, we had become partners.

I touched a long, raised scar on the underside of his forearm, the line too smooth under my fingertips.

"Dumb mistake from my first year at the forge," he said after a minute, his voice quiet.

I couldn't stop looking at that scar. And thinking about what he had said back in the kitchen, about how living in Klamath Falls had been a little lonely. Kai Andrews—the kid everyone loved, who had always seemed surrounded by friends, last I knew him—living alone with his dog, gathering scars.

I examined the rest of his arms more closely, the spiderwebs of evidence of smaller past hurts that criss crossed his skin. They made something stir in my gut, his weathered arms. Arousal, but also something...protective. Concerned. Something sharp and unexpected.

A gust of wind rattled against the window, breaking my concentration. I glanced outside at the flurry of white crashing against the panes.

I bit my lip and looked back at Kai Andrews.

Maybe, just while we lived in this snow globe of an

apartment, I could pretend I actually could be his partner. Someone who got to examine his scars, who got to worry about his dangerous job, his mental state. And then I could lock it away in my memories, like Baja, like the Olympic rain forest. An epic adventure I'd gone on once. Something to write about, one day.

It didn't sound like such an awful idea, in the moment.

I leaned down and kissed him.

I was utterly obsessed with Kai's lips by now, so soft and full, erotic little pillows. I licked across his bottom one, tugged at it with my teeth before delving my tongue into his mouth again. His arms fell from the lamp to wrap around me, and I smiled.

"You really are bad at this," I said against his lips. I sat up to remove his arms from my back, returning them to the headboard.

"Sorry, sorry," he breathed out.

"Do you have any ties or anything? If, you know. You're okay with that?"

"Yeah. I am." He cocked his head toward the closet to my right. "Over there."

I jumped off him and opened the closet, a spike of adrenaline coursing through me at getting to rifle through Kai Andrews's stuff. His closet was neat, pretty spare, mostly full of t-shirts. Sneakers and boots were lined up on the bottom, sweaters and sweatshirts folded up top, and—*yes*—some flannels and Henleys hanging next to the t-shirts. He was absolutely a bisexual lumberjack in his heart and maybe I'd make him try some of those on for me later.

Almost hidden, over to the right, existed an exceedingly small selection of formal wear. Including one hanger with exactly two ties.

"Wow. What selection."

"I don't dress up a lot," he huffed out. "I don't, you know, have to wear a suit to work under my PPE."

"You have to wear PPE to your job." I considered both ties. "That's hot."

"Is it?" he asked. "It's more just hot, like, literally."

I decided on the coral pink tie—obviously I did—and climbed back over Kai on the bed.

"You sure about this?" I asked, holding the tie in my fist and searching his face. I was new at this, too, but I knew I could hurt him if we didn't do it right. "We don't have to do any of this."

"I want to," he said. "I promise I'll tell you if it doesn't feel good."

I liked everything about this sentence. Promises. Feeling good.

I closed my eyes briefly. Focused. And began.

Wrapping the silk around his wrists felt like such a precious thing. I gave him some slack, which allowed him to sink back onto the pillow just a bit more comfortably. Did my best attempt at knotting it firmly around the base of the lamp. It was possible I'd watched a few YouTube videos about knots, at various points in my life. I silently cursed myself for not having more practice—I wanted Kai Andrews to think I was brilliant at this too—but I thought I did a decent job.

I locked my elbows around his chest. Stared down at him.

"Kai," I said. "What do you want?"

I watched him swallow, the lovely angles of his throat.

"Isn't this about, um, what you want?"

"Yeah," I answered. "And I want what you want. To start with."

He licked his lips. Hesitated.

"I want you to tell me," I reiterated. In what I hoped was a half-commanding, half-affectionate kind of way.

"Okay." Another gorgeous swallow. He closed his eyes before he said, "God, I want you to suck me off, Aiden."

My dick reacted to that exactly as I thought it would.

"That's acceptable. Only if," I leaned down toward his mouth again, "You keep talking to me. I want you to tell me every single thing that feels good, Kai. I want details."

"Oh god." His eyes scrunched closed even tighter, and I was both a little worried I was pushing him too far, and a little distracted by how cute it was. "I'm not always good at…" He cut himself off, blinking his eyes back open, his face smoothing into determination. "No. Okay. I'll try."

I ran a hand over his stomach, and he twitched.

"You don't have to do anything you're not comfortable with. Seriously."

"No, it's good. Just…don't laugh at me."

"I won't."

I sealed my own promise by giving him one last kiss on the mouth.

And then I got down to work.

I WANTED to touch him so badly.

Which was the point of all this, the tie wrapped around my wrists, and everything. It probably wouldn't have felt so impactful, being deprived of something, unless you really wanted it.

But as Aiden made his way down my body, and—oh, *fuck*, he didn't waste any time, *god*—I wanted to shove my hands in that curly hair. I wanted to caress my thumb down his cheek. And—

"Talk to me, Kai," he pulled off to remind me, which

felt torturous, since he had just started, and it had felt so incredible. But, right.

I released a puff of air I'd apparently been storing up in my lungs.

"Well," I tried. "Your mouth feels really fucking good, McCarstle."

He hid his face in my thigh. I realized he was muffling a laugh.

"Good start," he lifted his head to say. "Maybe try to sound a little less aggravated next time, if you could."

Oh.

My.

God.

I had just made him promise not to, and he'd broken that promise immediately, but...I had made McCarstle laugh. I had *finally* made him laugh, and it was...by being so horribly inept at dirty talk.

The worst part was, I *wasn't* aggravated. Or, okay, at least not in an annoyed way. Any hint of annoyance bled out of me when I decided to slide down my kitchen wall. When he wrapped this tie around my wrists, the silk smooth and taut against my pulse points.

I wasn't annoyed. I was overwhelmed with how...sexy I felt. With how free I felt, laid out like this at Aiden's feet, all the control in his hands. I felt hyper sensitive, turned on as all get out, like I could explode at any moment—and more deeply at peace than I'd been in years, all at the same time. It was...it was a lot.

And I didn't want to fuck it all up by sounding like an idiot.

It didn't help that the man who had just had my dick in his mouth was a fucking poet. He could probably make a blowjob sound majestic. I wasn't sure I'd ever made *anything* sound majestic in my life.

"Hey." Aiden leaned up on an elbow, looking at me with a hint of concern. His other hand was still wrapped around the base of my dick, and he rubbed his thumb along the side of it, almost absentmindedly, which was both oddly sweet and far too excruciating a sensation, especially for how on edge I was right now. I wanted his mouth back there, hot and encompassing and obliterating. "Kai, sorry. You don't have to talk. Or do any of this at all, really. I can untie—"

"No." I swallowed, and my head began to clear. All I had to do was talk. It didn't have to be deep. It didn't have to be sexy. I could do this, for him. For me. "Don't you dare. And I'm not aggravated. This is...wonderful."

His hand stilled, his face softening.

After a few seconds, I added, "But you're going to have to go back to what you were doing, or I might die."

His mouth twitched, and something sparked to life behind his eyes. They looked...mischievous. It was a good look on him.

"I don't know. I might have to take my time, now that you said that."

I groaned, tearing my gaze away from him and banging my head back against the headboard. But he moved his hand, his whole fist this time, thank god, and stroked me slowly, carefully, perfectly.

I took a few deep breaths and closed my eyes. Swallowed. And I talked.

"I've never had someone tie my wrists like this before. *Ugh*, your hand feels so good when you—yeah, like that. Shit. Anyway, I like it, the tie, even though my neck feels a little awkward. It feels like...something I shouldn't want, but it actually feels amazing, like such a relief, like—"

His mouth was suddenly on me again, and I hissed, my hips bucking involuntarily.

"Sorry," I babbled. "I might not be able to control that. The fucking your face thing. Is that okay? It just feels so good. I don't know—"

Aiden's hands gripped my hips, hard, his fingernails digging into my skin, sharp little crescents. I gasped, opening my eyes and looking down at him. My hips bucked again at the sight of him there.

"Fuck. I don't know if that means yes or no."

He moaned around my dick, and I...was going to take that as a yes.

"Okay. Fuck." I sunk against the headboard again, fisted the ends of the silky tie in my hands. I didn't know how to summarize out loud how I felt about what he was actually doing. Other than: *God. Yes. Uuunnnnggggggghhhhh good.* And Aiden McCarstle deserved better words than that. So I opened my mouth and tried to remember what I had been saying.

"I like it, like this, the way we're—*oh.* That. *Aiden.* God." He did this swirly thing with his tongue, and I closed my eyes. Tried to focus. "Being like this, it makes me feel like I'm...yours."

Aiden paused mid-motion. Didn't make a peep. Which I probably should have expected. Good lord. I had to start saying different things, so he wouldn't pull off again and walk away into the snow.

"I like your hair," was what came out of my mouth next, which probably wasn't any less embarrassing, but it was the first thing that sprung into my mind. "And your collarbones. And your mouth."

He resumed his movements, a little more aggressively this time, and I shivered in relief.

"You are...very good at this," I managed. God, sentences were hard.

And then, as if to prove to me that he could be even

better, he dropped his hand and took me in deeper. I felt myself hit the back of his throat.

"Oh shit, Aiden," I almost yelled. "I don't want to hurt you. I—" Oh, but I was fucking his face again anyway. His hands gripped my hip bones again, where he'd dug into me before, but now he just held on, pressing into their hurt, firm and reassuring.

"Damn. Damn, Aiden," I whispered. "You can't stop doing this, ever." And soon, "I'm close. I'm so close, Aiden."

He swiped a thumb over my skin, as if telling me it was okay. And that was all I needed.

There were sparks behind my eyelids, relief everywhere else—the back of my thighs, the crook of my toes, the crunch of my shoulders. I hadn't come so hard in a long time, and it felt almost surprising, like it was a new sensation. My back arched off the bed, arms clenching around my head, my brain a peaceful blender of waves. I didn't talk then. Didn't want to. Wanted to just sink here inside these feelings as they expanded around me, stretching into my fingertips, wrapping around my chest.

I felt Aiden pull off, felt him kiss the inside of my thigh, and I liked that, wanted him to keep doing it. Wanted him to cover my body with his, so he could share in my afterglow, so I could spread it from my skin to his.

Instead he crawled over me and fell over onto his side on the bed. I could barely see him anymore, since my arms were in the way. But I could hear his heavy intake of breath, in tune with my own.

We laid there a moment, two.

And even though my body felt light and tingly, my brain still recovering, the next words I spoke felt heavy somehow, like they were wrenched from my gut.

"Tell me something real about you, Aiden."

10

AIDEN

I COULD BARELY SEE his face, just that otherworldly sculpture of his shoulders, his triceps framing his head. I was pretty out of my mind with desire, a kind of deliriousness creeping up my spine, so it took my brain longer than it should have to even register that Kai had said something. I only kept hearing him say *I like your hair* inside my head and wanting to dissolve into euphoric laughter. No one had ever been so cute during an erotic moment in their entire life.

"I'm feeling kind of like I've said a lot of things, and..." Kai tried again when too much time had elapsed without me saying anything. I tried to sober myself up, focus. Except then his tongue reached out to lick across his bottom lip, and I stared at it too long, still in a bit of a daze. I had always liked looking at Kai Andrews, but looking at him now, up close and personal, all the little details bared to me, it felt a bit like I had discovered a new species. Every single thing he did was interesting. "I don't know," he finished. "I want to know something about you."

This was completely fair, of course. And it was probably just the adrenaline in my system, and the fact that most of my brain cells had migrated to my dick, but I didn't even feel that mad about it. Kai had already given me so much. We were in the snow globe. I could tell him things.

"I hate grad school," I said.

"Yeah?" He tried to turn his head to see me, but he was mostly still looking at his own armpit. I laughed a little.

"You doing okay?"

"Actually...my arms are kind of falling asleep?"

I sat up immediately. Untied him. His head hit the pillow with a satisfied grunt as his arms fell limply to his sides. Eyes closed, he rolled his neck a few times. And then he simply laid there and smiled.

"Tell me if they don't feel back to normal again soon, okay? And your neck's all right?"

"Yeah. It's good. And I will."

"Oh shit, Kai," I said, the realization hitting me. "We should have maybe established a safe word? I think?"

Kai laughed, but a jab of embarrassment punched through my sex-haze bliss. I was apparently pretty bad at this, too.

Kai's laughter faded as his face turned thoughtful, a comfortable moment of silence stretching. He chewed a bit on his lower lip before he said, "Is it dumb or weird to choose Jack?"

My heart did a little flippy flop thing. Of course Kai would choose his old dog.

"I always felt safe with Jack," he added.

"Absolutely," I said. "Not dumb or weird at all."

I settled back on my side and wrapped the coral tie around my own hand, like I was a boxer getting ready for my next punch. Trying not to think too much about

Klamath Falls Kai. About Jack. Trying to hold on to the sex haze. I held my wrapped fist to my mouth.

"Why do you hate grad school?"

Right. We were still talking about this, then.

I thought about where to start, how to explain it to Kai.

"Well, I'm not very good at it, for one." I grinned into the silk, my daily misery suddenly seeming a little funny when I looked at it from here, naked in Kai Andrews's bed. "I've started at least five different theses and...I don't think any of them are great, or groundbreaking, or even unique. Like—" I grinned even harder. "Who cares? I'm not solving world hunger or anything here."

This had become a mantra, something I chanted to myself on the days when I felt particularly angry and disenchanted, with school, with my classmates, with myself.

Who cares? Who cares? Who cares?

"I don't think you have to solve world hunger to still be doing something meaningful," Kai said. I ignored him, because I had already moved on to the second worst part of grad school.

"And I have to teach." I started laughing in earnest now. "I have to teach undergrads and..." I shook my head. "Kai. I am *so bad* at it."

He had been staring at the ceiling as I talked, which was great; it made talking easy. But now he turned toward me again, a frown on his perfect face.

"I'm sure you're not as bad as you think you are."

"Kai." I looked at him over my fist. "I am awful. Legitimately. Which is especially dumb because a lot of writers get advanced degrees so they can *keep teaching.* But I get so nervous before every class, and then when I'm actually in front of the room, I only feel like an asshole up there, and I just...it's bad. It's so bad. I am not built to lead other human beings."

He cracked a smile at that. A very small smile, but still.

"Why are you there, then?"

I sighed, my own grin fading. Another fair question.

I flopped onto my back, taking my turn to stare at the ceiling.

"Because it seemed like a good idea. And I didn't have any other good ideas. I kept thinking, as senior year of undergrad rolled around, that I'd figure it out, what I was supposed to do next. I got an internship at Tin House, and I thought that would help, or give me connections or something, but..." I wondered how dumb and self-important this was all sounding to Kai. "I still needed more money to start paying student loans. So I started working at this bakery, along with the internship, and I thought...I'd figure it out when the internship ended, if I wanted to go into editing, or something, or I'd get an agent and they'd tell me what to do next, but...soon I was just, you know. Working at a bakery."

"Did you like working at the bakery?"

"Yeah. It was a nice break, actually, just going somewhere and doing hard work and then going home and not worrying about...you know, being more of a genius than all the other geniuses."

"That makes sense."

"But it started to feel, last year, like everyone else was moving forward and I wasn't." For some reason, much to the consternation of my dick, I was still talking. "And I could tell any time I talked to my parents that...they weren't judging me, exactly, but were sort of like, okay, we let you get that writing degree; now it's your turn to get a real job. And...maybe I, like, don't even know what a real job is."

Shit. I was starting to sound messy. And like a child again.

"So I applied for grad school because it was what the writers I knew and admired most were doing, and it felt like something I could say to my parents, to people who asked what I was doing with my life. I'm pursuing an MFA. It's...something."

"Something you hate," Kai said.

"Yeah." I shrugged. "But I'll get through it."

An awkward pause lingered between us.

There was more I could have said. About how I thought, as with my internship, that grad school would bring me connections, bring me into this world of bright, interesting people, that I could be a part of something.

And maybe I had made some connections. Maybe I was doing fine.

But I couldn't help feeling like nothing felt like I had thought it would. That I felt weirdly disconnected from everything and everyone. And I couldn't tell if it was because everyone else were assholes, or because I was the asshole. Either option made me equally depressed.

I was meant to be moving *forward* with my life. And yet, the only people who I felt truly understood me, who I only ever wanted to be around, were Penelope, who had known me since I was a seventh grader who made extremely poor fashion choices, and Niall, who I'd broken up with a year ago, who I hadn't talked to in six months.

"Anyway, that all probably sounded really whiny," I said, feeling a little horrified, wishing more than ever that I had stuck to my Only Sex plan.

"No, it didn't. It sounded honest."

"Yeah, well. Now you know. I'm not actually brilliant. Just...scared of everything."

Another beat of silence, just as horrifying.

I was right on the cusp of opening my mouth to say, "Anyhoo, let's go back to fucking," when Kai said, "You're also a dog walker."

A laugh that sounded more akin to a bleating sheep escaped my chest.

"What?"

"You said when people ask what you're doing with your life, you can say you're pursuing an MFA. But you're also a dog walker."

I covered my face with my hands to quell my laughter.

"Oh my god. Getting burned by Kai Andrews. Adding that to my list of things I didn't expect to happen over the last twenty four hours."

"It's not a burn! I love that you walk dogs. God, that has to be stressful sometimes, right?"

"I…" I shook my head in disbelief, feeling like a sillier human being than ever. "Yes."

I should have led with dog walking, actually. There was no reason why I should have told Kai about my grad school angst, but I could have told him about the time Mitzi almost lost an ear from an off-leash dog at Thousand Acres, how there was still a blood stain in the back seat of my car from when I'd rushed her to the emergency vet. Or the time Stanley Tucci slipped his collar and almost ran straight onto Powell Boulevard and I'd thought, this is it. This is the day I kill a dog and have to give up on life. Or when Buster knocked over some trail mix from the kitchen counter in his excitement of seeing me and I had to tell the owners I had no idea whether he'd consumed any raisins or not.

Kai probably would have cared about those stories more than my internship at Tin House. But what was done was done.

He didn't make any other ridiculous comments, and I

counted down the minutes until it felt socially acceptable to bring up fucking again, when he spoke.

"I'm scared of my mom's house."

Now I turned to him, and he faced the ceiling again.

"I'd always wanted to come back home, eventually, but when she passed away last year...I have to clean out her house. My old house. When the job came up at the port a couple months ago, it gave me the final push to finally quit my job in Klamath Falls and come back. But..." He blew out a breath. "I've only been inside it twice since coming back. I've driven by it a lot more than that, but I keep making excuses. I needed time to get settled into the apartment here, get used to the new job. But I know I'm just avoiding it."

Jesus.

"Is there anyone else helping you? Does it need to be cleaned out right away?"

Kai shifted one of his arms to rest behind his head. I tried to not focus on how incredibly sexy this pose was, considering he was telling a much more important story than any of the junk that had just fallen out of my lips.

"My aunt's helped a little, and she's offered to keep helping. But she's also gently told me it's my job, that I'd regret it eventually if I didn't do it. I know she's right. And Dad moved to Bend after Mom died. He..." Kai's lips thinned, his forehead creasing. "He's actually doing okay, I think, or as okay as he can be. But he knew he had to leave, find somewhere new to grieve. He took what he wanted to take from the house, and now I think he's...done."

I knew absolutely nothing about Kai's dad, or his aunt —or about his mom, for that matter—but something hot flared in my chest. It didn't seem completely fair, that Kai would be left to this monumental task all alone.

"And you don't have any siblings or cousins or anything that could help?"

"Yeah, no siblings. Only kid. I do have some cousins...huh, I actually hadn't thought to ask them before. Maybe I'll do that, if it truly is overwhelming. And Pen has offered to help. But...I actually do kind of want to take it on by myself. I just need to find the courage to, you know. Do it."

We were in this weird space where I had just shoved his dick down my throat, and yet...I didn't know if I could hug him.

It probably wasn't a good sign that I really, really wanted to, though.

"Anyway," he turned his head to me. "I feel like it's my turn to do something to your dick now?"

A strangled laugh escaped my throat.

This was a weird fucking night.

"If you're up for it."

"I am. Sorry if I ruined the vibe."

"No, I started it." I thought about this, and shook my head. "Actually, you started it by asking me to talk. Now you know what a bad idea that was."

"I disagree." He smiled at me, and it was a little sleepy, his eyes half closed. My chest squeezed. "But yeah, maybe you should punish me."

I closed my own eyes. This was quite a step up in dirty talk, from his *I like your hair* beginnings. But I wasn't sure, exactly, what Kai meant by punishment, if he had actually meant it that way. I had liked tying him up. Applying small pressures here and there. Hearing him gasp. But...whatever he was imagining didn't feel right, right now.

"I just want to fuck you," I said. "If you're okay with that."

He inhaled a quiet but sharp breath.

"Yeah," he said. "I'm okay with that. Only..." he hesitated. "I don't want to be on my knees, if that's okay. I want to see you."

I breathed out, a worrying patch of tenderness flaring underneath my sternum.

"Yeah, that's okay, Kai. Do you have lube? And condoms?"

"Yeah. Top right drawer of my dresser."

I hopped to, and good god. I stared at the lube sitting among his rolled socks, and...Kai Andrews actually did have lube. I didn't know why this surprised me. I also did *not* want to think about whoever else Kai Andrews had used this lube with.

"Do you want to tie me up again?" he asked as I crawled back between his legs. And while my erection had flagged during the whole I'm Bad At My Life/Kai Has to Clean Out His Dead Mom's House discussion, my dick perked back up at the question. Which he had asked so innocently, so genuinely. Kai Andrews was too pure for this world.

"No," I shook my head. "But," I shoved up his knees, "you're going to hold these."

"Right," he said, grabbing hold immediately, and...fuck. I didn't move an inch for a good minute, just staring at his thighs, at his whole body, exposed to me. And his face looked so goddamn *calm* about it.

When I had pictured fucking this man, back in the Moonie's parking lot, and all the years before that, I always imagined it rather frenzied, hard and dirty, hot and desperate. But now that the moment was actually occurring, all I wanted was to be gentle.

And before I could get too in my head about it, I gave it my best try. I leaned forward and planted a kiss on the inside of his thigh. I moved my hands anywhere I could touch him, from his ass to the space behind his knees, to his hips, his stomach. I left dumb little kisses everywhere, all before I'd even popped open the cap of the lube. And when I did lube up a few fingers, I was nuzzling his balls, his thighs, like he was a very precious puppy. I was being ridiculous, basically, but I couldn't seem to stop myself.

Either way, we were both pretty worked up by the time I removed my fingers. Without the pressure of having to talk, Kai's body had relaxed, and he'd been emitting all sorts of noises—sighs, moans, grunts—with every touch, every shift of our bodies, that made me feel like I was out of my head. Breathing deep to steady myself, I took my time getting inside him. Watched his face for any sign of discomfort. Watched his face just to watch his face, really. Waited for him to adjust. Absorbed the spine-tingling, barely-there little groans he was making now.

And when I finally slid out and back in, I moved almost excruciatingly slow. Wanted to savor it, stretch it like taffy.

Again, I was being a bit ridiculous. But I imagined every slow, deep stroke somehow soothing the hurt he'd shown me on the patio at Moonie's. Easing the burden of painful responsibilities he bore.

Which, of course, was pretty much the complete opposite of Only Sex. But Kai Andrews deserved to be soothed.

And I'd obviously already lost the thread here a while ago.

"McCarstle," he eventually ground out, his face dewy, cheeks stained the most delicious shade of red wine, "You're killing me. God."

"Something you need, Andrews?"

His fingers were starting to slip on his thighs. He threw his head back onto the pillow with a groan.

"Fuck, Aiden. Fucking *fuck me*."

So apparently Kai *could* get bossy.

But the man made a good case.

I shoved his hands away, taking over, shifting his knees up even further, adjusting my own stance. And then I did as he asked. It took me embarrassingly little time, in fact, to get back to stark carnality, to fast and sweaty and loud and inelegant and so, so fucking good. I was too close to coming, too fast.

So to make sure he came first, I gritted out the only command I'd uttered in this whole sequence: "Touch yourself."

He did, almost before I'd even finished speaking, crying out in relief when his hand made contact. He came within a few strokes, making a mess of himself, and being able to truly study him, his beautiful open mouth, was both everything I'd ever dreamed of and like nothing I'd ever actually expected. I felt this rush of so many things: gratitude, for being able to witness it, and a touch of shame, like I didn't deserve this moment of intimacy with him. Sorrow, that this was probably the last time in my life I'd ever get to see it. Words were crashing through my brain, the exact right words I would use to describe everything about this, if I had pen and paper, if my hands weren't otherwise occupied with Kai's skin. I was low-key mad I knew I'd never be able to write them down in time, before I forgot, before they flew out of my brain.

Seconds later, I was gone.

Usually I came down pretty fast, especially if I was by myself. And to be real, by myself was the only action I'd gotten in a long time. Within minutes, I could be back to watching TV or reading a book, like nothing had even happened, like my orgasm had merely been a passing yawn.

But tonight, even after the last shudders of my release faded, even after I'd pulled out, it felt like I was still half in it. I walked to the bathroom, disposed of the condom, got a towel to wipe Kai down. And the whole time, my body was still buzzing, my mind still in a cloud, floaty and overly aware of every single sensation. Like if Kai so much as brushed my skin I might come all over again.

Except he didn't. By the time I slid under the covers, he'd moved over to the other side of the bed, his body barely covered with a sheet, eyes closed, arms resting like dead weight at his sides. He looked conked out, and when my body weight shifted the mattress, he didn't move to curl into my side, or wrap me in his arms. Which I appreciated. I often felt claustrophobic and overwhelmed by too much cuddling, right after—it had caused some hurt feelings, more than once, with Niall—and especially with the weird, tingly, overstimulated haze I was in, it probably would have made me implode.

So instead we simply laid on our backs, side by side, and waited for our heart beats to return to normal.

At least, that was what I did. I was pretty sure Kai was asleep, had probably been asleep since I'd crawled back onto the bed.

But then I heard him shift. Felt his hand glide along my palm. And next thing I knew, we were holding hands.

And it was perfect.

"Shit," he said. "I feel like I could sleep for a hundred million years."

"Yeah," I mumbled. "See you then."

Before I lost consciousness, I tried to think of what I'd say tomorrow morning. I felt alarmingly tender toward Kai now, and didn't want to be a total jerk about it, the fact that me and Kai Andrews as a *thing*, as a unit outside of this bedroom, still didn't actually make any sense in my brain. No matter how wonderful—and weird, and a little confusing—this night had been.

Maybe I'd just say that. *This was wonderful. Let's never do it again.*

And for all I knew, maybe Kai would whole-heartedly agree.

Except as my body sunk further into the darkness, I had a harder time remembering why, exactly, that was what I wanted.

Maybe my brain just needed to work a little harder. Maybe this *could* make sense.

After all, Kai had said it himself. Even though I'd been trying to forget it ever since he'd said it, because it had felt like such an outlandish thing to say—

Tonight, Kai Andrews had been mine.

All I had to do was believe it.

I could be better, braver than I was in high school. Right?

I fell asleep before my brain found the right answer.

11

KAI & AIDEN

If it weren't for Aiden McCarstle's bony elbow jabbing me in the side when I woke up, I would have sworn the previous evening was a dream.

It was still snowing. And now that there was daylight behind the grey-white clouds, the world outside my window seemed overblown, too bright, filling the bedroom with an ethereal glow. Like maybe it *was* just a dream.

But then McCarstle moved, his elbow jamming into my ribs a bit deeper, and yeah. Nope.

His head was turned toward me, the arm that wasn't stabbing me curled up under the pillow. I let myself stare at his face for thirty seconds—I actually counted, inside my head—at the way his curls fell over his forehead, at the smattering of freckles across his nose that were so faint I wasn't sure I had ever noticed them, until now. He looked peaceful when he slept, skin smooth: not even a hint of scowl lines.

I crawled quietly out of bed when my thirty seconds were up. Anything more than thirty seconds seemed fool-ish. Even those thirty had probably been ill-advised.

Last night was the first time anyone had stayed over in this apartment with me.

And I had liked it, waking up with Aiden McCarstle's elbow in my side.

I grabbed my phone from the side table and padded over to the window.

The world looked so quiet out there, everything a blanket of white. No tire marks on the roads, no footprints on the sidewalks. Not a soul around.

Aiden wouldn't try to leave in this. Right?

A low groan sounded behind me, the shifting of sheets. My pulse pounded, and I googled frantically anyway.

It hadn't *seemed* like just a night of fucking, last night. But I still couldn't trust my gut completely when it came to McCarstle. He was too stubborn, too skittish. Even though my heart kept floating around my body in a dumb soup of hope every time he looked at me in that intense way he looked at me sometimes. Every time it seemed like he had lowered his shields. Every time he used my name in casual conversation—*Kai, I am so bad at it*—like we were friends. Every time he touched me. And he was really, really good at touching me.

Still. It would not surprise me if he *did* try to leave in the middle of a blizzard and I never saw him again.

I scanned the local headlines on my tiny screen. My hope soup swirled around my veins in triumph. I opened my mouth as soon as I heard him roll off the bed, before he reached me, before he had a chance to speak first.

"The buses aren't running."

I turned to see him rub a hand over his face as he approached me at the window, eyes still half asleep. He garbled out some indecipherable, rusty sounding syllables, which I think amounted to, "Say what?"

"There was freezing rain earlier this morning," I

explained. "And now more of this—" I gestured behind me, to the furiously falling flakes of white—"which means snow on top of ice. It sounds like the roads are impassable. The whole transit system's not running until it at least warms up some."

"Oh." Aiden looked dazed, like his brain was still processing what I'd said.

But—*but*—he didn't look disappointed. Or upset that he was stuck here with me. At least, not yet.

I had to do something, before his face changed. Because suddenly my mind was whirring, excitement racing along my skin at the prospect of all I could do with a day of being snowed in with Aiden McCarstle. If he didn't close himself off again. If we could only continue what we had started last night. Not just the sex, but the talking, too. The laughing.

He just needed to stay.

I couldn't wait for his command this time.

I dropped to my knees, and without preamble, grabbed the base of Aiden's morning erection in my hand, gliding my mouth over the tip.

Aiden startled, leaning a hand onto the glass of the window to steady himself.

"Jesus, Kai." He sounded more awake, now.

But he didn't push me off.

So I kept going, even though it was completely lewd, doing this right in front of my window, two minutes after he'd woken up. But I didn't think anyone could actually see us up here, and the rest of the city was still cooped up inside anyway, and...the world just seemed so pretty, right then, everything hushed and pure. I had been desperate to keep him here when I started, but the more I went on, it felt right, somehow, just our bodies and the whiteout outside, the quiet only broken by Aiden's harsh breaths.

He threaded his fingers through my hair, curled his fingers around the short strands until I felt the tug at my scalp. The gentle pressure of it felt so good that I had to pause for a moment, my eyes fluttering shut, a small moan escaping my mouth. Which only made Aiden tug harder.

Dizzy, I took in a few breaths before I continued, my want mounting with each passing second. Remembering the command Aiden had given last night, that had almost tipped me over the edge through words alone, I moved the hand that wasn't wrapped around the base of Aiden's cock to my own erection, moaning again as I touched myself.

"Kai," Aiden breathed. "God."

I let his approval wash over me, shivered a little in its glow.

He said my name again a moment later, his command broken up by heavy breaths: "I want you to come," *pant*, "same time." *Pant*. "Wait until I'm there too."

I stilled both of my hands, taking my own minute to breathe.

"Yeah," I whispered. "Okay."

I was already on the edge, unsure if I'd actually be able to hold myself back much longer. I upped my speed on Aiden's end, and soon—

"Now," Aiden wheezed.

My vision was a blur of Aiden's skin and the bright world outside, dancing against the black that hovered at the edges of my mind. And then—fuck—I—

I was choking, tears streaming down my face. I coughed, my throat making embarrassing sounds as I struggled for air. I tried to apologize, but I couldn't make my vocal cords work, and—

"*Shit.*"

Aiden sank onto the floor, pushing me down with him, so I was suddenly against the window, the cool glass against my back soothing. Aiden ran a thumb across my cheek-bone as a few errant tears leaked out, his face creased in concern. It would have been sweet to see, if I wasn't still trying to recover from being a mess.

Apparently I wasn't able to swallow while in the throws of my own orgasm. Which I likely would have realized from the start, if I wasn't so ready to do whatever Aiden McCarstle asked.

"I'm so sorry, Kai. What a dumb thing to—I'm just still half asleep, and—"

"It's okay," I managed, blinking, airways seemingly cleared.

His thumb moved down to the corner of my mouth, and I became aware that—oh god—his spunk was defi-nitely all over my face. And neck. And mine was—who knew. I was trying to decipher whether this was all horri-fying or sexy when Aiden leaned in and kissed me.

It was the opposite of how our first kiss had been last night. This kiss was slow, but purposeful, his hands cradled around my head with surety and command while his tongue worked lazily inside my mouth. It was this gentle, languorous exploration that felt...decadent, almost. The way morning kisses should feel.

The panic I'd felt when I first awoke, sure he would try to leave, bled away, the ache in my chest from my choking fit subsiding. I pulled him to me, stretched my legs around him to keep him there. Rubbed circles on his side. And even as he continued to kiss the hell out of me, I swear it was like he...soft-ened. Like all of his sharp angles became more malleable, an easiness he hadn't yet let me see. A funny kind of kitten, purring in my lap. Bony, lanky, but a kitten nonetheless.

"Shower?" I asked once he finally pulled away, once I recovered my breath.

"Together?" Aiden sat back on his heels. A part of me wanted to reach out and bring him back to my lap, but I knew I shouldn't press my luck.

I nodded, and he shook his head.

"Showering with other humans is always a bad idea."

I frowned.

But I knew the day was going to be okay when that was all it took—just one frown from me—to make Aiden sigh and say, "Fine. But I get to say I told you so when it's the worst."

And, okay. Maybe it was sort of the worst. One of us was always cold, and anything I thought would be sexy only turned out awkward, water splashing into our eyes and our mouths. And I'd had enough choking for one morning.

Still, it was worth it. To feel clean, and to see Aiden smile, which he did a lot, every time he got to stand under the showerhead and watch me shiver.

We toweled off, and I threw on some sweats and an old t-shirt. Noticing him standing uncertainly in the corner, I rooted around my dresser and offered him the smallest set of clothes I could find. He scowled.

"Those are going to be too big."

I shrugged. "You can wear your Moonie's clothes again, if you want."

Grumbling, he took them from my hands.

Giving him privacy, I padded to the kitchen, yawning as I went. I turned on the coffeemaker, rooted around the fridge. Brought out eggs, a block of cheddar, bacon. I'd just put the frying pan on the stove when I heard Aiden enter the room.

I slid a mug of coffee his way as he slumped onto a stool at the kitchen island.

"Shut up," he said, followed immediately by, "Thank you." He wrapped his hands around the mug.

I managed to keep it together—mostly—until I turned back to the stove.

The clothes *were* too big on him. And I loved it. The sight of Aiden McCarstle, sitting at my kitchen island, wearing my clothes, unexpectedly made me want to explode. I hoped he couldn't tell from the back of my head how big I was smiling, that the cheesy scrambled eggs I cooked were the only ones to witness my sheer delight.

We ate in a comfortable silence, other than the satisfied groans Aiden couldn't seem to keep inside when he first chomped down on a piece of bacon, first shoveled the eggs into his mouth. The happy hum as he refilled on my coffee. I just sat next to him, trying not to glow too much.

I took our plates when we were done, ran them under hot water. I was rinsing the frying pan and thinking about what we should do next—Aiden probably wouldn't want to go out into the snow and, like, make snow angels, or anything, but maybe I could carefully pressure him into it—when suddenly he was behind me, arms wrapped around my stomach, mouth at my neck.

The pan slid out of my hands.

Almost involuntarily, I sunk back into him, my entire body doing this *woosh* thing that I was learning happened whenever Aiden was too close and it wanted him to take over. One of his hands snuck underneath my t-shirt, the other traveling lower, palming me over my sweats while his lips dragged over my neck, and god. I shuddered, everything suddenly running hot in my system, burning to the surface of my skin. I was so lost to him like this. He had to know.

"Kai," his breath tickled the back of my ear. "I want you to fuck me."

Okay. Well. Right. Okay. No snow angels then, for now.

I turned off the tap.

~

KAI TURNED. I pushed my hips against his, gripped the sink behind him. Everything in this kitchen was so new. Shiny and flawless.

"I've, um." He blushed, staring at my mouth. "Never done that."

It was especially cute seeing Kai this bashful right now. Like he hadn't sucked me off when I was barely still awake, whilst vigorously jerking himself off, a mere hour ago. Like he hadn't been practically gleeful about me tying his wrists to his headboard with his own tie last night. Like he wasn't remarkably free with his body, in this fascinating way that was both shy and confident all at once.

It must have been a combination of the morning orgasm and the breakfast he'd just made me, which had tasted like the best thing I'd ever had in my goddamn life, that made me so...okay, right now. More than okay, actually.

I was stuck in Kai Andrews's apartment, a pair of his too-big sweatpants tied around my waist, one of his faded t-shirts slumping around my collarbone. The snow appeared to have no intention of stopping. I had no idea when I'd be able to leave.

And I wasn't freaking out at all.

It was like any desire to fight against this had swiftly disappeared in the muted, early morning light, in the blizzard that closed us in here together.

Maybe it *was* the blizzard, actually, that was magically calming my brain. It wasn't just Kai Andrews's mouth, or his cheesy eggs. I no longer merely had to imagine we were living in a snow globe.

This was a full blown snow day.

And responsibilities didn't exist on snow days.

I understood why Kai liked ceding control to me. Like he was right now, practically limp in my arms. It was freeing, not having the option to leave. I felt weightless, trapped in time.

I didn't have to decide jack shit about anything, as long as it was still snowing.

"I would tell you what to do," I told Kai now. "But it's okay if you're not into it, seriously."

"No, no," he reached around me, grabbing my ass, like he'd done at Moonie's last night, losing some of his shyness. "I want to. Tell me what to do."

I kissed his nose.

I was a nose kisser, apparently, on snow days.

"Take off all your clothes and wait for me on the couch."

He did as asked, in good haste, as I was coming to expect. He listened to all of my rough instructions, changed positions easily when requested, until I could truly feel the power of those soccer star thighs, those welder's shoulders, and it was so good I nearly lost consciousness.

He laid his head on my chest afterward, while our bodies cooled down. I didn't mind the contact, for now. I felt tender and bruised in all the right ways.

"Wow," he said. "That was…"

"Fantastic," I finished.

"Yeah."

"Thank you for that. And for breakfast," I added. "And, you know, the stuff before that."

He laughed a little, a puff of air dancing across my nipple.

"Snow days are the best."

"They really are," I agreed. This was even better than when I was in high school. Apparently non-stop orgasms with a remarkable person beat out reading alone in my room and listening to Radiohead. Who knew.

"Aiden?" Kai asked after several minutes had passed. I blinked, realizing I had been spacing out, watching the snow out of his living room window. His voice was tentative, and for the first time all morning, I tensed. "Can you read me one of your new poems?"

"Oh," I laughed. That wasn't what I had expected, at all, but the answer was easy. "No."

He pushed off of me. Leaned down to pick up his t-shirt from the floor. Sighed as he pulled it over his head.

"Yeah." He reached for his underwear. "Figured that'd be the answer."

Shit. I scrambled up into a seated position, startled at how sad he sounded. Or disappointed, or something. Which was not at all how he should sound, after what we'd just done. It kept ringing in my ears with wrongness.

This had been a fucking excellent morning. If I had somehow ruined it, before we even hit lunch, I'd actually hate myself.

I thought about him sneaking looks at my poems during pre-calc. Talking about looking for me at Barnes & Noble. My stomach twisted. He kept...doing this. Saying things that pulled me in different directions. Routes I didn't know how to navigate.

I had a bunch of poems on my phone, and several more memorized. I knew it was nice, that he cared about them. But it felt like too much. It felt like when I'd stared a little too long at the scars on his arms last night.

And workshopping poetry was what I did out there, beyond this shiny, window-filled apartment, in ugly classrooms filled with ambition and harsh lighting. I wanted this one timeless day outside of all that, where I didn't have to worry about metaphors or cadence or meaning or worth. Where I could just be.

I didn't know how to explain all of that to Kai without hurting him.

He stepped into the bathroom. Awkwardly, I waited for my turn, cleaned myself up, put his t-shirt and sweatpants back on. He had left a new toothbrush on the counter for me to use. I stared at it for at least three beats too long.

When I returned to the living room, Kai was in the kitchen, brewing another pot of coffee, so I perused the bookshelf in the corner. It was half full of books, half full of framed photos, trinkets and mementos. The books were mostly mysteries and non-fiction, a bunch of manuals on welding and construction and woodworking.

"Coffee's fresh, if you want more."

I turned. He stood a few feet away, blowing on the top of his steaming mug, his other hand in his pocket. He looked casual, and fine—and hot, because he always looked hot—not hurt or sad or disappointed anymore, but a weird pressure to be a good person pushed at me from behind my ribcage anyway.

"I could read you other people's poems," I blurted. "If you wanted." I lifted a hand, let it drop. "I could tell you about some of my favorite poets. It's...easier, sharing someone else's words."

Kai looked at me over his coffee. A corner of his mouth curved steadily up.

"I would love that," he said, and my stomach danced a needless little jig. *He didn't fuck it all the way up!*, it shouted to my spleen.

I opened my phone and did a quick Google. And then

I read him an Ocean Vuong, right there, while we stood across from each other in his living room.

When I was done, he said, "Thank you."

And he walked over and kissed me.

His phone rang a minute later—his aunt calling, making sure he was safe in the snowstorm—and as he walked away to take it, I went back to nosily looking around his apartment. Pretending the moment hadn't shaken me, hadn't felt overwhelmingly intimate.

Easier to keep staring at his bookshelves, the art on the walls, that view out his window. By the time Kai returned, shoving his phone in his pocket, I almost felt normal again.

Almost.

12

AIDEN

We were sitting in front of the window, passing a bag of pretzels back and forth and talking about snow memories.

"We've never been particularly close, Jackson and me," I said, passing the bag back to Kai. "But whenever there was actually a good snow day, when we were kids, he'd pull me through the neighborhood, right in the middle of the street on this old sled."

Jackson always felt a little bit like Superman to me on those days. Pulling me just fast enough to be thrilling, not scary.

"I think it always felt so wild because the street was this dangerous space every other day of the year, where you had to look both ways, that you couldn't cross without grownups. But on snow days, it was ours."

The time for lunch had approached and fallen away. We'd discovered Kai had little in his kitchen that *wasn't* bacon and eggs, so we'd decided to simply wile away the day with constant snacks.

After a few moments of comfortable quiet, Kai said, "I

still can't believe you've lived here your entire life and have never been skiing."

I shrugged, grabbing a pretzel. It didn't surprise me that Kai was a skier. Even if a true snowstorm like this in the city was rare, Mt. Hood, a skier's paradise, was only forty-five minutes away. But it had always seemed like a hobby reserved for the cool, rich kids, and I struck out on both of those qualities.

"I didn't say *never*. Pen's family took me once, freshman year."

"And?"

"And I don't see the appeal of purposely hurtling yourself down a mountain. And it was fucking cold."

Kai grinned in delight.

"It's also fucking *exhilarating*."

He went on, recalling his favorite Mt. Hood stories, gesturing with his hands, smiling and relaxed. I simply sipped my water and watched him, my own dopey smile on my face. Talking about my older brother had left me feeling weirdly sentimental.

It must have been the sweetness of that nostalgia that pulled my brain away from the details of Kai's story, about the time he and his friend Dylan, who I vaguely remembered, had tried snowboarding and "almost died approximately fifty times." While Kai laughed at his memories, my focus faded away, consumed instead with this vision: sitting inside a ski lodge, Timberline maybe. Writing and reading around the fireplace, sipping hot cocoa. Surrounded by strong pillars of warm timber, Pendleton rugs, deep, ancient chairs. Waiting, content, for Kai to wander in, cheeks rosy from the slopes, snow clinging to the tips of his wind whipped hair. His lips would be cold against mine as he leaned in for a kiss hello.

And then we'd sit together for a while. I'd buy him his

own hot cocoa. And eventually, he'd go back to the great outdoors, and I'd crack open my book again.

I blinked. Kai was still chuckling to himself, shoving a pretzel in his mouth. I hoped his story was over. I hoped I hadn't missed any cues where I was meant to jump in with a response.

Either way, enough storytelling for now.

I stood, scratching my elbows.

"Do you have any games?"

Kai looked up in surprise.

"Oh. Um, yeah, actually. I think."

Brushing pretzel dust off his hands, he walked to a closet in the small hallway by the bathroom. I peered over his shoulder.

"I have—"

"Boggle." I reached over him to grab the square, dented box from the top shelf. "We are totally Boggling, Andrews."

He sighed.

"We both know you're going to kick my ass at that."

"Maybe."

I did, in fact, kick his ass, most of the time. I spent the first half hour trying to tamp down my excitement about the Boggling, lest I appear too much like the hardcore nerd I obviously was. Or maybe the happiness coursing through my veins was simply relief at having something to focus on that made sense. Like letters and words and beating Kai Andrews. Fuck ski lodges.

Kai did, to his credit, triumph a few times. He looked so proud each time that it was difficult to keep myself from catapulting across the table to cradle his face and pat his hair.

Still, after over an (incredible) hour of Boggling, he flopped back against the couch, hands over his face.

"Aiden," he said into his fingers. "I know you're enjoying this, but if I have to Boggle with you one more time, I may scream. Just to let you know."

"Cool." I stood, stretched out my back, and promptly picked up the coffee table we'd been playing on. I moved it to the side, revealing the lush rug underneath it that I'd been tickling my toes on all day. "Take off your clothes and lay down."

Frankly, beating Kai at Boggle had gotten me rather riled up.

He let out a small gust of air when I pinned his arms above his head. He had been smiling to himself as he undressed, but when I looked down at him now, like last night, his face was a picture of perfect calm. Like he was at home here, with his wrists trapped underneath my fists. Like he trusted me.

And right then, I felt the same. My Boggle adrenaline bled out of my system, and I only felt fucking serene.

I ran my fingers over his scars again. I had made him tell me, earlier, more about exactly what it was that he did at the port, even though I knew I wouldn't understand a word of it. He'd shown me some videos of him doing welding stuff real good. They were all super dark and looked like nothing but random moving pieces of hot metal to me. It looked dangerous, and difficult. Kai looked very excited about all of it. It had been super dreamy.

I leaned down and nipped at his nipples. He sucked in a breath. I loved making Kai suck in a breath.

I decided then to take my time. Because time was the one thing we had today. Because I wanted to.

Slowly, meticulously, I licked and bit my way around his skin. Touched, listened. Caressed all the way down to his toes. Learned him, better this time than I had before. His hardness, so much muscle and bone, but his soft places, too. The inside of his thighs, right above his knees. His hips, where they curved into his ass. The sweet spot where his neck met his ears. His mouth.

It felt like the closest I'd ever come to physically manifesting a poem.

"Aiden," he eventually whispered, voice ragged. "Please."

He had never moved his arms from where I had originally pinned him, not even once. He was getting so much better at this. I was, too.

But when I paused to really look at him, he looked wrecked. Mouth open, taking in these shaky gasps of air. Eyes glassy. Like he was barely keeping it together.

I wanted to eat him alive. I rested my forehead on his chest instead, took a second to compose myself.

And then I took him in my mouth.

He came to pieces in minutes.

Thank god we still had lube and condoms nearby from earlier, because I was pretty incoherent with need after that. It was fast, and hot, and Kai was just so good and open, and I had no words at all in my head, this time. Only raw sensation and connection. It was like I forgot myself entirely, and...I couldn't remember the last time I forgot myself entirely. That I hadn't been consumed with trying to find the right words. It felt like free falling. Too much, and just right.

I was shattered, afterward.

I barely had enough energy to tap his wrists. And then I curled myself on top of him, my head on his chest, a leg draped over his thighs.

"McCarstle," he whispered. "Thank you." I felt his nose nestle into my hair.

I knew, then, that the line I had tried to draw in my head was blurred for good. The line where we were just two people stuck inside, enjoying each other. His hand ran absently up and down my shoulder. I listened to his heart beat.

It didn't feel like just a snow day, anymore.

We laid there for a long time. I listened to his breathing return to normal. I tried to find equilibrium.

I grasped it, finally, when I felt him shift, the arm that wasn't around me going behind his head. I realized suddenly that I knew what was coming next, could practically feel whatever question it was making its way from Kai's brain to his mouth, and it made me want to laugh. Which helped me get out of my head.

Kai just really liked asking probing personal questions after orgasms. Like spilling secrets around a campfire. Camp Sex and Share. It was very Kai.

"What's the one thing you want most?" he asked. "If you could accomplish one thing, the rest of your life."

I turned my head even further into him, to hide my grin in his chest hair. Helplessly, I squeezed my arm tighter around his side.

Surely, he knew my answer to this one. It seemed so obvious—and so annoying—in my own head.

"I want to publish books," I said.

Kai just kept rubbing my shoulder.

"Tell me more. About what your books would be like."

Ugh, Kai, I thought. Grinned a bit more. But I gathered my courage. Wanting, for some reason, to be a good camp participant.

"I've had poems published here and there. But I want a whole book full of them, where I could organize them by theme. And someone could have it on their shelf and open it up to a random poem whenever they wanted, and then put it back on the shelf until the next time they needed another one. I want the pages to be slightly yellowed.

Something soothing and nature-y on the cover. A really good serif font."

I almost laughed at myself, once I finally shut my mouth. Except I didn't want to laugh at myself. I only felt like I should. And I knew Kai didn't care either way. So I didn't.

"And...I want to travel more. See more of the world to write about."

"Mmm," he hummed, a rumble on the side of my cheek.

"What about you?" I asked back. "What do you want?"

"I want a house," he said, without hesitation, "with a view of Mt. Hood. A decent amount of land. Maybe out in Estacada or somewhere."

"That sounds nice," I said. Because it did.

I imagined his port job, with the risk of all that hot metal, probably paid well. I imagined a house with a view of Mt. Hood was actually realistic for him.

My chest squeezed, not exactly in jealousy, but in admiration, maybe. For having dreams that were actually accomplishable. I couldn't wait for him to get that house. To be happy.

"Yeah. I'll have to figure out something at some point, about what to do next. I can't do my current job forever. It's too physically and mentally demanding. I've seen the guys who've done this for too long. I don't want to...break myself."

Immediately, almost unconsciously, I tightened my hold on him even more.

"But I'll figure something out. So I can still get the house, one day."

I almost dozed off once silence settled over us again. Thinking about Kai's house. Thinking about my bisexual lumberjack, traces of gray in his hair—fuck, he would look so good, even more weathered—rocking gently on a porch swing.

And then he said, "You should quit grad school."

My eyes blinked open.

"It's...not that easy," I eventually got out.

"I think it probably is, though."

I tried to picture going home for Christmas in a few weeks, telling my parents I'd quit school. That I had no plan.

I wanted to go back to my lumberjack Kai dreams.

"I need the loans to survive right now," I managed. "I can't exactly live on dog walking pay."

"So get another job. Go back to the bakery. You can work at the bakery and still write."

I was quiet.

"Sorry," Kai said after a minute. He blew a breath into my hair. "I don't have the right to tell you what to do with your life."

"It's okay."

I pushed off him, though, finally.

I walked into the kitchen. Filled a glass with water from the tap, drank the entire thing in one go. Found some tortilla chips.

When I walked back into the living room, Kai hadn't moved. He was still lying on his back on the rug, a small, concerned crease between his eyes.

I sank onto the couch. I didn't know how to explain it to him. Or even to myself, really. That his suggestion that I quit school wasn't an inappropriate thing to say. I wasn't angry.

But it felt scary when Kai said it because he'd had the courage to say it out loud before I did. And now that *someone* had said it out loud, it was going to live in my head forever.

One thing I did know was that I wanted Kai to stop looking at me like that. Like something had just gone wrong, like he thought I was mad at him. Because it wasn't him I was mad at at all. So I got back up and looked around for my phone. I finally found it in the bathroom.

And I read him a Mary Oliver, to be nice.

FOR DINNER, we had cheesy eggs again.

And it was, honestly, perfect.

Hours had passed since the grad school conversation. Hours spent sharing odd little high school memories. Sharing more poems. Staring out at the snow and the darkening sky, doing nothing. Pen had texted, assuring us she was home and doing fine. I felt so warm and content by dinner that afterward, I suggested watching a movie. Kai chose some Captain America thing, something safe and full of loud noises. I curled into his chest on the couch, let him play with my hair, because...because it felt good. Because I had lost the line. I hadn't been careful at all. I had stopped being careful, probably, the minute I first touched the scar on his arm last night. The snow was starting to taper off, but the world outside was still quiet. I fell asleep halfway through.

Kai jostled my shoulder during the credits. He leaned down to grab the remote from the coffee table, clicked off the TV. It was so dark and still then, both in the apartment and in my head, the glow from a small lamp on a side table the only thing lighting the room.

Kai stood, reached out a hand. He led me out of the living room.

There was something about walking toward his bedroom this time, the second night in a row I'd be resting my head on his pillows. We'd mostly lazed away the hours today in the living room and the kitchen, so going back to the bedroom felt...it was silly, and hard to describe, but it felt both special and familiar all at once. Like this was our routine now. Retiring together. Like lovers.

We were halfway there when the power went out.

The kitchen light clicked off, all of the shiny appliances whooshing a quiet sigh as they powered down. The snowy night outside Kai's windows, which had been illuminated in the street lights, went dark, too.

We froze. After a second, Kai turned and kissed me. It felt like the most romantic moment of my life, and I was glad we were standing in the pitch dark, because suddenly I felt deeply embarrassed. About just how carried away I'd let myself become.

After stumbling around for a bit with his phone's flashlight—I didn't dare try to use mine; the battery was almost dead—Kai unearthed one of those big candle jars from somewhere. Lit it and put it on his dresser. It was something cinnamony, rich and sweet.

I swear I meant to seduce him some more. Fucking Kai again by candlelight probably would have been a pretty fine way to finish off this day.

But it turned out my body had had enough of that. I remembered getting under the covers, Kai murmuring something in my ear about going to the bathroom, being right back.

And then, by accident, I fell back asleep.

13

KAI & AIDEN

I KNEW, instinctively, the moment I woke up and realized the space beside me on the bed was cold.

Everything was cold, really. I could hear the heat humming to life, but the power must have only come back on recently, because it was freezing in here.

But nothing felt quite as cold as Aiden McCarstle, sitting on the opposite corner of the bed, pulling on his socks. His black and white striped sweater was back on, his dark jeans. The clothes he'd borrowed from me yesterday were neatly folded and stacked on my dresser.

He stood, and I could feel it even before he turned to look me in the face. That restlessness was back. And when I did get to see his eyes, they were wide, slightly panicked, like they had been when I first sat down at Moonie's two nights ago. Like they had looked almost every time I ran into him in high school.

"Right. So," he said, clearing his throat.

He turned and left the room.

Dammit.

I hissed when my feet hit the floor—shit, it was cold—

and threw on a pair of sweats before following him to the kitchen, before he could leave without saying goodbye.

Even then, within the space of however many seconds it took me to do that, he'd already put on his coat and shoved his feet into his sneakers.

Dammit dammit *dammit.*

"Aiden. I don't think it's even safe to go out there yet."

He took his phone out of his pocket and waved it at me.

"Just checked. Buses are running, with chains."

I leaned against the kitchen island, crossed my arms over my chest.

"You could at least stay for breakfast." Except, wait, I'd used the last of the eggs last night. "Or a cup of coffee, at least. We should talk."

"Yeah, um." He ran a hand through his hair. "No thank you."

I swallowed to silence my growl. I knew there was probably no point even trying to argue with him. His shields were back up. He'd let them down for a precious twenty four hours with me. Had let himself be happy for a day.

And now, he was as closed off as he'd ever been.

But I didn't find his cageyness charming anymore.

He held all the control here, and I knew it. But this wasn't a control I had granted. This was a control that wasn't fair.

"Look," I sighed. "I know this—" I made a gesture toward my apartment, toward the winter world outside the window, "was intense. And probably not a totally normal way to start a relationship, but I—" Aiden's face went entirely blank at the *r* word, but fuck it—"I'd like to see you again, Aiden. I..." I faltered, wondering exactly how much I should put myself on the line here, how much of my heart I should give him when I knew, rationally, that he didn't want it.

But the irrational part of me wanted to tell him anyway. That I'd hoped moving back home would help me heal, finally, after Mom's death, but I'd only felt out of sync ever since I came back. And that I hadn't felt truly at home here—in this apartment, in this city again, in my own life—until Aiden let me sing ELO. Until he kissed me. Until he stayed here with me, and read me poems, and kicked my ass at Boggle, and treated me like I was important. Like we were important to each other.

"I had a wonderful time," I finished.

Aiden looked away, closing his eyes for a moment.

"I did, too," he said eventually, voice strained. "But I'm sorry; that's all it was, okay? A wonderful time. I got to live out a fantasy—"

"I'm not a *fantasy*, Aiden," I bit out, anger flashing in my veins. "I'm a human fucking being."

But it was like he didn't even hear me.

"And you got…" He went on, waving a hand limply through the air. "You got another notch on your bisexual belt."

I sucked in a breath. An awful, tiny moment of silence transpired before I could respond.

"That's a really shitty thing to say, Aiden."

"Yeah, well." He ran a hand through his hair again and sighed. Like he knew it was. But he'd said it anyway.

"Bye, Kai."

And he left.

I watched him walk through the door. Watched the lock snick shut behind him.

Felt the loneliness swoop back into the apartment, filling it from corner to corner, before Aiden had even made it down the hall.

I breathed in through my nose in bitter frustration. Pressed a hand to my neck, where he had bitten me two nights ago. I had looked at it in the mirror yesterday, the purple mark unmistakable. Knew Alice at work would give me shit on Monday. It still felt tender under my fingers.

I knew there were other patterns left on me, down my arms, my sides, my hips. The scrapes and indentations of his fingernails, his teeth.

The asshole got to walk out of here scot-free.

But I'd be carrying his bruises for days.

I HADN'T BEEN PREPARED for the sun.

It had been so bright when I woke up, the sky so shockingly blue.

I had looked over at Kai's slumbering body, his skin golden in the light, his hair rumpled, his mouth slightly open as he slept. He was more perfect than he'd ever been.

And all I felt was wrong.

I slipped and stumbled on the melting snow, the surface beneath my feet icy and uneven. The world was still quiet out here, everyone else still wrapped in the safety of their homes, no sidewalks shoveled yet. Just walking the block and a half to the bus stop was a journey that left me out of breath, a freezing damp seeping into my sneakers, my entire body uncomfortable and clumsy.

It'd take the city days to dig out from this. My car was likely still buried in the Moonie's parking lot. Even if it was accessible, I wouldn't trust it to make it through these messy streets. I'd have to bus it all the way home. Which, especially if the buses were chained, would take forever.

Forever to sit with my wet feet and my sad brain. I didn't even have a book with me to read. And I'd used the last 1% of battery life on my phone double checking the buses were running.

I was almost to the bus shelter when I bit it. One wrong step and I was on my back on the ice, almost smacking my head on the corner of a bench.

Ow.

I laid there a minute, blinking into the sun, the breath knocked out of my lungs.

I pictured Kai leaning over me, reaching out his hand. Wrapping me in his arms. Warming me up.

I already missed him.

And suddenly, simultaneously, as the sun bore into my irises, I missed Niall.

I always missed Niall, in a way.

I pictured what Penelope would do if I told her. *I think I'm in love with Kai Andrews. But instead of telling him that, I said some real mean stuff and then ran away.*

"Aiden!" She would say, eyes flaring, smacking me in the chest. "You march back in there and make it right *right now.*"

Niall would look at me and laugh. "Of course you did, you sad bastard."

And then he'd help me up and we'd go nurse some cheap beer and feel sorry for ourselves.

With a groan, I maneuvered to my side, managed to push myself to a sitting position.

Falling in love with Niall had been so easy. We met in college, when I had been able to reinvent myself. To only show him the parts I wanted. When I had felt, for the first time, understood, seen. Surrounded by people like me, people who had always felt different, who had never fit in high school, who had yearned to break free and live a life that was new and uninhibited. Where we could all be ourselves, all of our incongruent parts, our wild, unstable minds.

We had gone to art gallery openings together, me and Niall, poetry readings, had stayed up too late, fucking and getting drunk on cheap wine. On road trips, we took pictures of each other with an old film camera he'd found in a thrift shop in Seattle. On the way to Baja, we'd sat on his friends' roof in LA, stared through the hazy night and pretended we could see the stars.

Looking back now, so much of our relationship had been a cliché. But it had felt beautiful, at the time. It had felt like I was finally alive.

And now, I was in stasis.

And while being wrapped in Kai's arms again would feel incredible, it also felt so much more complicated. Our lives were still so far apart. He was clearly dealing with his own, much more serious shit. And Kai didn't know the me Niall had been able to see. He only knew gawky, socially inept Aiden McCarstle from high school, when I'd been crawling out of my own skin every day. He only knew the Aiden McCarstle he'd met at Moonie's two nights ago, inexplicably angry and disillusioned with his life. He only knew the worst parts of me, and I didn't understand why he'd still given me so much kindness. God, I was exhausted with myself half the time. It seemed cruel to subject a shining light like Kai Andrews to that exhaustion for longer than a day.

Except...I hadn't really felt exhausted with myself, yesterday.

The bus rumbled up to Kai's stop. I stepped on, clinked the change I'd scraped from the bottom of my bag into the payment box, since my phone was dead. I dropped myself into a seat up front. My body felt heavy, tired.

I leaned my head against the window.

Penelope was going to be so mad at me.

I suddenly, desperately wanted to go back to Kai's apartment and do it differently. I didn't know why I'd said anything I said, especially that bisexual belt bit. Jesus.

Except...I did know. I had needed to be the worst version of myself, say the most hurtful things, so that he'd stop being so wonderful. So he'd let me go.

But as the bus made its way through the slush and ice, regret soured in my stomach, warring against everything else already muddled there.

I didn't want Kai to think I was a shitty person. Even if I was. Even if it shouldn't matter what Kai Andrews thought of me.

I wanted everything to be different.

God. I could lose myself in him, probably.

The only problem was, I already felt so lost.

If I lost myself in him without finding myself first, I might disappear completely.

PENELOPE BLEW up my phone the next day.

Aiden Logan McCarstle. What did you do to Kai Andrews???

He just texted me that you and him probably shouldn't hang out together anymore

?????

Look, I know it was shady, not telling you he was going to come to karaoke, but he's been going through a hard time lately, and needs friends, and...I don't know, I always thought you two would get along

Even though I know you were always so weird about him in high school, but I thought that was just because you had a massive crush on him

But I thought we could all be cool now that we're adults!!??

Were you a jerk??

Did you at least get home okay?? Kai says he's safe at home but I know your car can't handle this shit

Sigh. Okay fine just text me back to let me know you're okay

I'm officially unconcussed, by the way. At least I think so. Not sure if that's the official term. Anyway I'm free to text is what I'm saying

I love you, even if you were a jerk

But you should text me back, you jerky jerk

14

KAI & AIDEN

I HAD to give Aiden McCarstle credit for one thing.

He helped me get off my ass and actually start taking responsibility for myself.

Even if it was just because I could hardly stand to be in my apartment the following week. Every room reminded me too much of that day. It even still smelled like sex the whole next day, and like him: constant reminders of all the places we had let each other in, literally or otherwise.

As soon as the roads were clear, I got the hell out of there.

My mom's house smelled the opposite: dusty and stale, a space lost to time. Except it felt a little less stale, and I felt a little less sad, each time I went back. I made a plan: one room at a time. Made to-do lists and notes on my phone. And I made piles. So, so many piles. So many trips to Goodwill. Ran my truck back and forth to the dump.

Guilt seized the back of my neck with each one of those trips. Would she have approved, that I got rid of that gravy boat? That stack of paperbacks? Almost every single item of clothing? Would Dad have been okay with it?

No, I knew Dad trusted me. Which was why he'd left it all to me. I knew she would have trusted me, too, but it was just as hard as I'd imagined it'd be, at least some days. Not being able to ask her.

What here was important, Mom? What do you want me to keep?

Some things were obvious. The photo albums, the kitchenware and pottery and jewelry I knew had been passed down. The quilts she had made by hand.

And then there were the piles that weren't just hers, but my own memories that lingered in this place. These decisions should have been easier, but I felt her presence even more, sometimes. Like when I threw away almost all of my soccer trophies. *Kai Andrews!* I imagined her saying, slapping my hand. *You worked hard for those!* I laughed when I discovered, in her bedroom closet, a box full of almost everything I'd ever made in shop class in high school. I winced at the rudimentary joints, how sloppy the weld beads were. But then I smiled, remembering what a badass Mrs. Robles had been, how instrumental she'd been in getting me my apprenticeship. How supportive she'd been of me feeling pretty positive that I was done with academic schooling once high school graduation hit. That I was meant to work with my hands.

A week after I met Aiden at Moonie's, I sat in my childhood bedroom and finally texted a couple of my old friends. I knew Lars and Dylan were still in town, or at least in nearby suburbs, but we had lost touch over the years. And it was an awkward thing, trying to re-establish relationships that maybe weren't even viable anymore.

But Lars had texted back immediately.

FUCKING ANDREWS, it's been FORFUCKINGEVER
Come play with us Sunday night, 6:00
We kick a ball around on the old Meadows field every week
Muddy as shit at the moment but still worth it

FUCK can't wait to see you dude

~

MUDDY AS SHIT was probably an understatement. Because even though the rain had returned, washing away most of the snow, it was still December, only a couple of weeks away from Christmas. So it was more like muddy ice, which was brutal.

But god, it felt good to kick a ball around again.

There were some guys I didn't know, friends of Lars and Dylan they'd found in the years since we last saw each other, but they all thwumped me on the back and welcomed me onto the field. I couldn't even quite remember, honestly, the last time I'd put on spikes, but I was wheezing within ten minutes. My feet were soaked, my legs streaked with mud even faster. I was shit, basically. And the guys let me know it.

I hadn't felt so happy since, well. Since McCarstle. But happy in a different way, a simpler way. A soccer field would never let me down.

Still, I kept thinking about Aiden, as the night wound down, as I sat on a cold metal bench with my old teammates to switch back into our sneakers, as we caught up on each other's lives. Maybe it was something about the adrenaline of the night matching the adrenaline I'd felt on the dance floor at Moonie's, or something about being around other people from high school. But if these guys were actually going to be my friends again, I suddenly wanted them to know.

"Hey," I said, grabbing a small towel I'd thrown in my bag, wiping down my face. "I want to tell you guys something."

"Shoot." Lars slicked his white-blonde hair away from his forehead.

"I sort of figured out something about myself when I was living down in Klamath Falls."

Dylan turned fully toward me, propped his chin on his fist, grinning.

"Do go on," he said.

I rolled my eyes, but laughed a little. "I'm bisexual." I shrugged. "Just wanted to let you know so it wouldn't freak you out, if I start dating a dude or something."

"*Have* you dated dudes?" Lars asked.

I shrugged again. "A little."

Lars let out a whistle.

"Damn," he said. "Impressive."

"Okay, so I have questions," Dylan jumped in. But then he frowned. "Wait. Am I allowed to ask questions? I'm trying to be less of an asshole."

I shoved his shoulder.

"Dylan. You were never an asshole. And yeah, you can ask questions."

"I know you said you only recently discovered this, but did you have any hints or anything, when we were in high school? Or like," he licked his lips, motioning with his hands, "was there anything we could have done as your friends that would've helped you feel more comfortable to discover it?"

"No, man. You were good. I was pretty clueless. I think that was all on me."

"Okay. It's just, Dakota's only two, but I want to make sure...I don't know, that he's comfortable being whoever when he grows up, you know? I'm trying to be less hetero-normative."

I smiled.

"I think if you're using the phrase 'trying to be less heteronormative' you're doing okay, Dylan."

"All right," Dylan breathed out, but he didn't necessarily seem reassured. God, being a parent seemed stressful.

"It is weird, though," I ventured. "Looking back at when we were younger, now that I know more about myself, you know?"

Dylan and Lars both gave knowing nods. Even though I didn't think either of them was queer, I guessed this strange sense of revised nostalgia might have been a universal feeling.

"I really don't think I knew it at the time, but now…" I swallowed. Tried to sound chill. Maybe getting this out would help somehow. "I think I had a little bit of a crush on Aiden McCarstle."

And Lars, but no way in hell I'd ever disclose *that*.

Dylan's eyes went wide. He leaned back, smiling again.

"Thank you," he said, holding out his hands. "This is the juicy stuff I was hoping for."

Lars's forehead creased, as if he was trying to remember. "Smart kid? Kind of a loner? But hung out with Penelope?"

"Yup," I affirmed. "That's the one."

"Wait," Dylan smacked my arm. "Andrews! I'm pretty sure that guy's still living around here! I see him on Pen's Instagram sometimes. Well, you probably know that too, I guess, if you and Pen are still close."

"Yeah, no, I know."

"Dude! You should ask him out! Oh my god. This is exciting."

"I think I'm good," I laughed. "But I appreciate your support."

And I was good. I mean, I was still a little mad at him. But it wasn't my job to make Aiden McCarstle grow up. If he wanted me, he could get my phone number from Penelope.

But until then, if the last year had taught me anything, it was that life was short. I had a house to finish cleaning, a life to pay respect to. And then I had to figure out, when I was done, how to put my childhood on the housing market.

My work was demanding. And now, I had guys to play soccer with a few times a month. I was contemplating getting a new dog soon. Something small and yappy and annoying, maybe, something the opposite of Jack. A dog that would make me laugh, a dog to make new memories with.

If whatever I had glimpsed with McCarstle never went beyond memories of the night I went to Moonie's and Penelope got a concussion, and the snowstorm afterward, so be it. It would be a good memory. And I wouldn't let Aiden's cowardice at the end of it all ruin it.

Because even when somebody left you, your memories were still your own to keep. You got to choose what to do with them.

WHEN THE ROADS cleared the week after I stumbled out of Kai's apartment, I finally got my car back from the Moonie's parking lot and tried to go back to normal life. Went back to school, workshopped a new poem, taught a string of horrible classes. Had trouble sleeping, sat up too late on my couch trying to push out words that wouldn't come. Watched my neighbors put up Christmas decorations, my block awash in sparkling lights and festive cheer.

Walked by the tree in Pioneer Courthouse Square. Watched the snow melt.

Missed Kai the whole time.

On Friday, I took Stanley Tucci and Buster to Chimney Park. I didn't usually take my clients to dog parks; they were too risky. But Chimney Park was the best dog park in the city, open and spacious, plenty of space for the dogs to run, less possibilities for fights.

I told myself Tucci and Buster deserved an afternoon at the park. It was a cold but beautiful day.

Another part of me, though, knew why I was making the drive all the way to this industrial part of the city, far from my own neighborhood.

If I went a certain way, it'd take me right past Moonie's.

I stopped on the way back, when the dogs were good and tuckered, their heads resting on their muddy paws in my backseat.

I crunched to a stop in the gravel lot. It was the middle of the day; Moonie's wouldn't open for hours. I was the only one here.

I stared at the excavators in the distance. Blinked into the sun.

Finally, taking a deep breath, I plugged in my aux cord and thumbed through my phone. And then I played it. "Aside" by The Weakerthans.

The first blast of the guitar felt like stepping into a hot tub. That initial step always a degree hotter than you expected, shocking no matter how you braced yourself. And then you adjusted, let yourself sink in, bit by bit. Realized you couldn't remember the last time your muscles had felt like this: indulgence and care.

I listened to it all the way through. Listened to it again.

And then I searched for ELO.

Stanley Tucci made a snuffling sound when the drum beats of "Mr. Blue Sky" kicked in. Glancing over my shoulder into the backseat, Tucci looked me right in the eye before opening his jaw for an enormous yawn. He proceeded to flop his head onto Buster's butt and promptly fell back asleep.

I laughed. I laughed because Stanley Tucci was cute, and I loved him. I laughed because the memory of Kai Andrews dancing around an empty Moonie's dance floor, hands flying out at his sides, made me laugh. I laughed because it was a funny song, and I loved that this was Kai Andrews's pump up song when he was a teenager, instead of something more hip or current or more...anything, other than what this was.

I laughed because it was one of those moments where everything seemed suddenly clear.

And dammit, I was an idiot.

There had been these puzzle pieces floating around in my head all week, constantly in the background as I went through the motions of my daily life. As I quietly processed everything that had happened during the snowstorm. As I kept on, annoyingly, missing Niall. As I dreamed about a Captain America with brown eyes and soft floral tattoos and a dopey grin. As I avoided phone calls from Pen.

And in the Moonie's parking lot, all the puzzle pieces clicked into place, crystal clear and certain.

I finally understood that all of the puzzle pieces were my fuckups.

But that maybe they were okay.

Maybe failing at grad school was okay. Maybe it was okay to fail at some things. Maybe I needed to learn that doing a thing because you're scared of doing anything else is likely never going to be the right choice.

I didn't think falling in love with Niall—and eventually,

falling out of love with him—had actually been a fuckup. But I understood it better now, sitting in the dusty Moonie's parking lot. It had been easy to fall in love with Niall because we had been so alike. Both full of the same big dreams.

I kept thinking, this last week, about reading poems to Kai in his apartment. Just him and me and the snow. We had never done anything like that, Niall and me, even though we both loved poetry. We would have found it corny, probably. Too earnest. We were so invested in being important in undergrad. Being the ones to change the world, to find the story that hadn't been written yet. Too stubborn and young to admit that it was the stories that repeated themselves, the ones you'd already heard before, that were the important ones, in the end.

I had needed Niall back then. To find somebody who saw me. To know I wasn't alone.

And it was possible, I realized now, that I had been comparing every relationship I'd even danced around since then to him. To that first big love.

But maybe what I needed now—no, what I *wanted* now—was someone who wasn't actually like Niall—or me—at all.

Maybe the differences between two people were actually the best parts of all of this. Maybe being different was the point.

And maybe loving someone wasn't about understanding everything about them. Maybe it only required loving their heart.

And I thought—I hoped—that maybe Kai Andrews didn't actually only know my ugly parts. Maybe *I* only saw my ugly parts. Maybe, like Penelope, Kai had in fact always seen me, even if I couldn't. Not just the gangly queer kid, or the insecure poet. Maybe he just saw me.

And maybe I'd never only seen the soccer star. Or the man who built ships with his bare hands. Maybe I'd seen that Penelope loved him, that everyone loved him, because he was so fucking lovable. Always giving everything and everyone his kindness and his generosity, even boys who scowled too much at him, and families who should have helped him better shoulder the burden of grief.

He had been right, of course, that morning. He wasn't a fantasy. He was better.

Maybe leaving Kai Andrews that morning was the biggest fuckup I'd ever done. The entire center of my puzzle. Without him, my pieces were merely an empty frame.

But maybe I could fix it.

Maybe I could strive to be the person Kai saw. The person he believed I could be.

Maybe I *could* be braver than I was in high school. Better than I used to be, but for real this time.

I unplugged my aux cord. Put the radio back on. Gave one more look back at Stanley Tucci and Buster. One last glance at Moonie's.

And then I put my car in gear and drove out of the lot.

THE NEXT WEEK, I showed up everywhere I was supposed to show up. I got to campus on time every day. Graded my last final. Wished my students and my classmates a happy winter break.

And then I walked to the registrar's office.

And I quit.

15

KAI

I'D MADE it to the attic.

Or more accurately, I had become irritated with the last bits of the kitchen—how many objects could one relatively small space possibly contain?—and decided to take out my frustration in the attic. For some reason I thought all the stuff up here would be old and boring, easy to sort mostly into the *For the Dump* pile. I could barely remember ever coming up here more than five times in my life; what could actually be that important?

Clearly, I wasn't very bright.

Because I'd only made it through one corner and already I was stumped. I sat on a dusty trunk by the tiny circular window and stared, dejected, at the box upon box of Christmas decorations scattered around me.

I thought I had been doing so well. Each day, the house looked less and less like a morbid time capsule, a museum Carol Andrews wouldn't have wanted, and more and more a simple, empty space, ready for someone else to fill with their own life.

But yet, here I was. Frozen by the most basic string of

Christmas lights. I wondered if it would be this, my mother's chipped collection of porcelain angels, that would truly break me.

I was so lost in thought I didn't hear the intruder until they were already clomping up the attic ladder.

In my startled haste, the only weapon I found in the near vicinity was a large wooden candy cane. I wielded it at my side like a sword, ready to use its cheerily white and red striped protection in whatever manner I had to, when Aiden McCarstle's curly black head of hair popped into the musty air of the attic.

"Jesus *Christ*."

I dropped the candy cane to the floor, leaning my hands on my knees.

"McCarstle." I breathed heavily. "What the fuck."

"Sorry."

I glanced up to see him blushing, blinking furiously.

"I knocked, but no one answered, and I figured that was your truck, and…" He scratched at the back of his head. "Your door was open. I'm sorry. Again."

I glared at him, my heart still thudding in my chest.

Except now I couldn't figure out if my heart valves were working overtime because he'd scared the hell out of me, or because now that he was suddenly in front of me again, I couldn't figure out what I felt. If I wanted to pummel the guy, or kiss him so hard he fell over. Because god help me, my blood was thrumming at the sight of him again. Maybe if I kissed him, I could conveniently knock his head on something on our way to the floor.

Whatever I wanted to do, it felt violent. And that surprised me, even though it shouldn't have.

"Why are you here, Aiden?"

"Um." He looked down, at where he was clutching a folded up piece of paper in his hand. And oh, geez. I knew, instinctually, that whatever was on that piece of paper would probably wreck me. Whether it was an apology or a declaration of undying love. Whatever it was, I wasn't ready for it.

But instead of handing it over, or explaining why he was here, he looked back up at me and said, "I quit school."

"Oh," I blinked, standing fully. "Okay."

And suddenly, the scales of my brain tipped much more firmly into the *just want to pummel him* column.

This was profoundly unfair, telling me something that he knew would make me feel proud of him, when I was still so mad at him. Because I knew now, that I had been lying to myself over the last two weeks. I had never felt non-violent toward Aiden McCarstle at all. I had simply shoved him away to the recesses of my brain so I could focus on other things, like this house, like getting my life back together. And now he was here, and I wanted to shake him.

What did he expect me to do, run toward him and wrap him in a hug? Pat him on the back for finally listening to himself?

"Anyway," he said, casting his eyes away again. "I just wanted to tell you that. And say sorry for what I said, before I left your apartment. You were right; it was a shitty thing to say. And I wanted to give you this." He shuffled forward and placed the slightly crumpled piece of paper on top of a box of Christmas tree ornaments. "And this."

And to my actual amazement, he pulled a flower out of his back pocket. A light pink peony. My mom's favorite flower. A perfect match for my tattoo.

That he had somehow procured in the middle of fucking winter.

He placed it on top of the paper. I couldn't stop staring at it.

Aiden stepped back, put his hands in his pockets.

"You can read it later, or never, or whatever." He swallowed heavily, staring somewhere in the direction of my feet.

And then he backed up, and left.

I heard him slither back down the ladder, walk down the hallway. Distantly, a minute later, I heard the front door click shut.

"What the *fuck*," I said again, out loud, to no one.

For too many long minutes, I stood there, motionless. Frustrated at myself that I hadn't stopped him before he'd slinked away, or at least said something more to him. Like "Hey," or "Stop," or, "Whatever's on that piece of paper, read it to me out loud, you coward." Or, "I missed you."

I blew out a breath and stalked to the window. Stared outside at the grey, miserable day.

Finally, I turned around and snatched up that dumb piece of paper. Sat heavily back on the trunk.

Our Favorite Songs, it said at the top.

And right underneath: *for you.*

I closed my eyes and breathed in through my nose. His handwriting was the same, a slanted scrawl. It made my lungs seize.

Once I'd reassured myself I could breathe, and wasn't going to have a panic attack over a single poem, I opened my eyes again. They raced over the paper, my brain working double time, the way it did whenever I got an important assignment back in high school, or another email from Mom's doctors, when she was sick. Rushing too fast to the end, uncomprehending, snatching words and phrases here and there.

And every single snatched word and phrase on this piece of paper melted my foolish heart.

Just as I knew it would.

At the bottom of the paper was a phone number. Next to that, an address for Sweetness Bakery. *Tuesdays through Saturdays, six to noon*, he'd written. And then, even smaller: *Get the sour cream strawberry muffins.*

I took another deep breath, fingers shaking, and started again from the beginning. I made myself read every line slowly this time. Made sure I took it in.

I read it through one more time.

And then I picked up my phone.

16
_____

Kai: what the fuck, McCarstle
Kai: why did you leave?

      Aiden: you mean this time, or the time I left your
      apartment two weeks ago like a real jackass?

Kai: this time.

    Aiden: right. Well, I wasn't sure if you'd want to talk to
    me. I wanted to give you time to read it, if you wanted,
    and then decide what you wanted to do next.

Kai: I read it.
Kai: and I would've liked it better if you'd stayed.
Kai: thank you. For the poem, and the flower

     Aiden: thank you for reading it. It's the first part of my
     ten step grovel plan

Kai: oh?

Aiden: yes. The other nine steps are surprises
Aiden: actually, no, the second step was, if you didn't hate the poem, asking you to dinner on Friday night
Aiden: but the other eight are surprises, I swear

Kai: I like surprises. And dinner.

Aiden: I'm sorry, Kai.

Kai: yes, you said that in the poem

Aiden: It might take me a while. To be better at this. I'm still...kind of learning. How to be better at this.

Kai: I think we all are, Aiden.

Aiden: the house is looking really good, by the way. I can tell how much work you've done.

Kai: thanks. Always nice to get compliments from your home intruders

Aiden: the door was open!!

Kai: actually...I had just gotten kind of stuck, before you intruded. I've been sitting here staring at these Christmas decorations for like an hour.
Kai: I don't know what to do.
Kai: anyway I hope at least three of the steps of your grovel plan are sex stuff

Aiden: wow way to ruin the surprise
Aiden: I was planning on the last five but we can negotiate
Aiden: but maybe, kai...you should put some up?

Aiden: the decorations I mean. like for one last time.

Aiden: and maybe that'll help you figure it out.

Aiden: or maybe that's dumb.

Aiden: I could help though, if you wanted.

Kai: it's not dumb. A little weird maybe, decorating an empty house, but not dumb.

Kai: I would like that.

Aiden: just tell me when.

Kai: I don't know if I'm ready. At least not today. But soon. Obviously. Since Christmas is in a week, and everything.

Aiden: do you remember George Lyman's christmas party, sophomore year? Pen dragged me along. You probably don't remember that I was there. But I remember you wore this wreath of holly on your head, and your cheeks were all red from the bourbon in the eggnog, and you were wearing this very nice, classy Christmas-y sweater, the color of cranberries. You were the prettiest Christmas decoration I'd ever seen.

Kai: fucking a, mccarstle

Kai: I...do not remember that. I wish I did.

Kai: I mean I remember Lyman's Christmas parties, but I don't remember ever seeing you at one

Kai: I wish you had talked to me more in high school, Aiden. Maybe it wouldn't have taken me so long to realize I had a crush on you

Aiden: lmaoooo KAI

Aiden: there is no way you had a crush on me in high school stfu

Aiden: the fact that we've had sex now is clouding your memories

Kai: no! I did!! I realized it practically the minute I saw you at Moonie's

Kai: My Bi Memory-Clarifying Muscles kicked in & I realized I'd been pining for you all along

Aiden: LOOOOLLLLLL

Aiden: KAI ANDREWS. you were dating Mei Qiang and winning state trophies for soccer; you were NOT pining for me omfg i'm dying

Kai: okay, SUBCONSCIOUSLY pining for you

Aiden: THAT IS NOT A THING

Kai: well excuuuuse me, Mr. Always-Known-I-Was-Gay High & Mighty!!!

Aiden: fuck you're cute

Aiden: i can't

Aiden: god i'm glad you don't hate me

Aiden: at least i don't think you hate me

Kai: McCarstle

Kai: hey

Kai: I'm proud of you for quitting school.

Aiden: thanks.

Aiden: me too.

Aiden: It's gonna make for some fun Christmas dinner conversation.

Aiden: What are you doing for Christmas?

Kai: Going to see my Dad, in Bend

Aiden: oh, right

Kai: I'm driving down on Tuesday. At least this is the second Christmas, without her, you know. I'm hoping it's at least a little easier than last year. But I don't know. Maybe it won't ever be.

Aiden: damn. yeah.

Aiden: you & your dad can start to make new traditions though

Kai: yeah. We'll get there.

Kai: anyway sorry I won't be around for any groveling plans that might have involved mistletoe or something

Aiden: psh please. I can do better than mistletoe

Kai: I'll be back for new years, though

Aiden: yeah?

Aiden: i would love to welcome in the new year with you, kai andrews.

Aiden: if you're not busy.

Aiden: and if i don't fuck up anything too hard before then

Kai: it's a date.

Aiden:

Kai: omg
Kai: i can't believe you just smiley faced me
Kai: if you had told me five years ago that aiden mccarstle would be texting me smiley faces I wouldn't have believed you

Aiden: shut up
Aiden: i can emoji

Kai: can you though

Aiden: 💥😡👎💀🙊💉

Kai: i mean it's a little weak, but acceptable

Aiden: wow
Aiden: if i was there, i would enact plan #9 right now
Aiden: which is more about you groveling than me, but i think it would work out for both of us

Kai: well, maybe you should be here, then
Kai: come back, mccarstle.

AIDEN STOPPED in the middle of the sidewalk. Pulled his coat closer around himself. Stared at his phone for a long, heart-fluttering minute.

Aiden: ...yeah? Right now?

Kai: yeah. Right now.

KAI PICKED UP the peony and made his way down the attic ladder.

Aiden: okay.
Aiden: shit. okay. Turning around.
Aiden: see you soon, andrews.

KAI GRINNED when he reached the kitchen, glad now he hadn't packed the whole thing yet. He found a small vase, filled it with water, stuck the impossible flower inside. Put it on the empty table.

It made the house feel like it belonged to Carol again, if only for one day more.

Kai walked to the front door. It was freezing outside, but he opened it anyway, leaning against the frame.

He waited until he saw Aiden McCarstle round the corner, curls flying in the wind.

His irritating poet.

Keeper of his favorite song.

He watched Aiden half-walk, half-run down the block, and he could see it, even from far away. The curve of McCarstle's lips, slightly crooked, like a secret unhidden. Better than a Mt. Hood sunrise. Better than a snow day.

Kai watched and waited as Aiden made it to the porch, as he looked up at him from the bottom of the stairs, biting his lip. Restless. Buzzing with energy. A Christmas song: full of ringing bells and unbridled hope.

Kai met him on the second step. Took McCarstle's face in his hands.

And swallowed his smile whole.

ACKNOWLEDGMENTS

Thank you to Maiga Doocy, whose comments on the first draft of this one were instrumental, and to Kate Cochrane, Jen St. Jude, and Manda Bednarik, whose feedback and friendship were also crucial.

Much gratitude once again to Em Roberts for the perfect cover, and as always, much love to my Fork Family.

Thank you so, so much to everyone who read *Sing Anyway* and took the time to share your love of it. It meant the world to me.

Finally, thank you to Kathy, who has, unfortunately, read some of my awful high school poetry, and fortunately for me, still married me anyway.

COMING SOON...

Meet me at Moonie's one last time in the Spring of 2022 for the last chapter of queer karaoke, wherein the butch bartender gets her happily ever after.

ABOUT ANITA KELLY

Originally from a small town in the Pocono Mountains, Anita Kelly currently makes their home in the Pacific Northwest, the perfect setting for wandering the woods, drinking too much tea, and dreaming of stories. A librarian by day, they write romance that celebrates queer love in all its infinite possibilities. They hope you get to pet a dog today.

∿

anitakellywrites.com

ALSO BY ANITA KELLY

Moonlighters novellas

Sing Anyway

Wherever Is Your Heart (Out Spring 2022)

Full-length novels

Love & Other Disasters (Out January 2022)